PRESENTS

I KNOW I WILL DIE IN THE SILENCE

THE BURRYMAN

A NOVEL BY CHARLES CAMPBELL

I Know I Will Die In The Silence – The Burryman

Copyright © 2020 by Charles Campbell

Cover Art: Francie Klopotic
Editor: Mary Frances Spires
Foreword: Francie Klopotic
Burryman Festival Consultant: Claire Taylor
www.valleyboypublications.com

ISBN 978-1-64921-263-4

FOR SETH, I LOVE YOU SON.

"I know I will die in the silence
with nobody calling my name."

State of Silence, Gin Wigmore

FOREWORD

BY FRANCIE KLOPOTIC

"Guilt is a curious creature; it burrows under your skin and sleeps. It sleeps and begins to grow as it slowly awakens." And when it awakens, it awakens the silence.

In "I Know I Will Die In The Silence – The Burryman," Charles Campbell takes you across the pond to South Queensferry, Scotland's Burryman Festival where past and present tangle in a stranglehold of guilt and fear. It is within these pages that you're introduced to the silence, and it is the silence that protagonist Scara Slayfield fears the most. Dark and foreboding, the silence is just a breath away. A heartbeat. It is a deep and brooding void that is ready to swallow you whole and capture you forever. Are you afraid of the silence? The book demands an answer, and you should be afraid…if Charles Campbell says so. When it comes to horror, anything Campbell writes should be taken quite seriously. From the Mrs. Fields trilogy to any of the stand-alone novels that Charles has written over the years, there is no one more capable of taking such an obscure Scottish legend and weave within it the threads of murder, guilt and psychological horror that make up the terrifying, silencing blanket of "I Know I Will Die In The Silence – The Burryman."

You will be haunted for weeks after finishing the last sentence. Charles and I became friends several years ago via Facebook when I was working on my first novel. He blazed forth on a path of writing that quickly established him as a powerhouse horror writer. Book after book flowed from his fingertips, and in 2016 he invited me to a joint book signing at the Book Tavern in beautiful downtown Augusta, Georgia. It was an honor to sit next to him as we met with friends and sold copies of our work. Our mutual love of writing solidified our growing friendship. So, when he asked me to read an early draft of the manuscript for the book you're holding in your hands right now, I jumped at the chance. I was thinking: "You're offering me a peek into the workings of Campbell's writerly mind? Of course I will read it, thank you very much!" It didn't take me long to plow through this story. From the first chapter, I knew right away that Charles had upped his game. Big time. His writing has taken a newer, higher road with deeper psychological twists that leave the reader breathless and clamoring for more with each turn of the page. How he achieved this leap is a mystery, as all of his novels are brilliant works of fiction. This book, however, is top of the mark and takes the cake. Or should I say the burrs.

A collector of my artwork, he asked me to create the cover art which is the highest honor for me as a visual artist. To design and make cover art for a writer the caliber of Charles Campbell was a thrill and a challenge.

How do I capture the essence of the story in such a way that will attract readers to pick up the book? How do I create a piece that reflects the essence of what the pages hold within?

And perhaps the most nagging question of them all: Do I have the ability to do this? Questions like these drove me into my studio with the determination to make it work. Merging his cover ideas with my creative thinking, we settled on the artwork you see here. I want to thank Charles Campbell for the opportunity to create this cover and to write this foreword. Such huge honors, both of them. I am thrilled to have been a very small part of what has made this book a huge success.

You are in for a treat, fellow horror fan. The Burryman awaits, so sit back, relax, and turn to page one. I guarantee you won't be able to put this book down until the absolute end. You will love some characters, you will hate some characters, but most of all you will be transported into the darkness in a way that only Charles Campbell can send you there.

This book is a key to the doorway of horror. Enter with care. Once you finish this story and emerge back into the mundane world, be sure to keep vigilant. Don't turn your back on the silence, lest you be drawn deep into its depths. That said, I will ask you again. Are you afraid of the silence?

Francie Klopotic
Visual Artist, Fiction Writer & Charles Campbell fan
Augusta, Georgia – 2020

CHAPTER 1

August 19, 2018: 11:15 PM – Augusta, GA

Johnny Pickens was tooling around with his phone when he saw her walking arm in arm with the man that stole his property. She was smiling at the man as she held his arm like only a lover would. This wasn't a walk between two friends; these two were much more and that didn't set well with Johnny.

Scara would scream if she saw him, of this he was certain, so Johnny kept his head down when he was in their line of sight. He felt the redness of rage fill his face. He was seething under the brim of his Atlanta Falcons ball cap. Broad Street in Augusta, GA was relatively quiet for a Thursday night seeing as how three of the four bars on Broad celebrated thirsty Thursday every week with watered down liquor and domestic drafts.

"I still can't believe I'm Mrs. Slayfield," Scara said as Jeff pulled her closer. They stumble-walked arm in arm down the sidewalk.

"Kira?" Jeff asked. Kira was his pet name for her. He mispronounced her name on their very first date and she liked the way he said it so she made him call her that.

"Yes," Scara replied.

"You are the wind beneath…"

"Shut the fuck up!" Scara shouted. "You know I hate that fucking song almost as much as I hate the fucking movie."

"I do know that, but just because you hate the lyrics don't mean it's not true."

Scara promptly held up a middle finger and reached behind his neck to pull him down for a kiss. They stopped under a street light and it was a lingering kiss; a kiss between two people in love; a kiss that exhilarated and scared them. They were certainly meant to be together.

"You want to go to the house?" Scara asked with a smile. Her black smoke lipstick was still moist from the kiss and this was making Jeff more than a little crazy.

"Kira, I absolutely want to go to the house," Jeff replied.

They hurried their walk to the parking lot near the Augusta Commons. Scara slapped a high five with the bronze James Brown statue as they moved past. Jeff followed his wife to the passenger side of the jet black Chevy Silverado and opened the door. He held her hand as she stepped onto the side rail and bounced her body into the passenger seat. Jeff jogged around to the other side and pressed the Start Engine button before his butt hit the seat. He was in a hurry to get this beautiful woman *back to the house.*

Three hours later.

Scara was tired but it was a good, worn out, completely satisfied tired. She threw on one of Jeff's XXL T-shirts before she rummaged around in the refrigerator for a late night snack. Great sex always made her hungry and Scara was famished. She left Jeff smiling and snoring in bed to grab a quick ham and cheese sandwich. She'd burned enough calories to have earned it. Scara was pulling the cheese from the tray when a noise made her pop her head out from behind the refrigerator door. It sounded like something was scratching glass. Scara took a quick glance over to Sheena's bed, she was curled up and cozy right in the center of it dreaming kitty dreams, so Sheena hadn't gotten out. It had been a couple of years since Sheena really seemed to want to go outside without prodding. So, it wasn't the damned cat, at least not their damned cat. Scara moved away from the refrigerator, not bothering to close it, set the Kraft singles down on the counter and stepped toward the closed kitchen window; a window that faced directly into the fenced in backyard. Scara could hear the patter of water hitting leaves and she was surprised by the rain. It was very light, barely audible even when she got close to the window. An irrational thought went in and out of her mind; she needed to wake Jeff. *Something was bad wrong. Something was bad wrong. Something was bad wrong.* The thought hammered her hard for a second or two and then Scara smiled at the ridiculousness of it. She flipped the light switch by the back door that lit up the deck. Scara's eyes widened and she screamed.

"JEFF! GET DOWN HERE! GET DOWN HERE NOW!!!!"

He took the stairs two at a time and was in the kitchen within six seconds after Scara first screamed his name.

"Babe, what is it?" Jeff asked. She saw the .45 at his side.

"He was out there," she answered. Her hands were shaking like a water logged Chihuahua.

"Let me catch that son of a bitch out there! Lock the fucking door!" Jeff stormed out the back door in only his boxers. The .45 was trained in front of him and he was ready to kill the motherfucker. She locked the door. Sheena was up and awake now. She had bolted from her bed and was hiding behind the living room couch. Scara heard more scratching, this time it was from one of the windows in the living room. Scara ran to the hallway closet and pulled the Remington shotgun from its designated spot. She removed four red shells from the open box on the top shelf of the closet and expertly loaded the shotgun. She had fired this gun many times growing up – her daddy made it a point to make sure she could handle a firearm.

Jeff was moving around in the backyard and he was at the far end. The backyard was a good acre of fenced in land.

Scara moved toward the living room window and the scratching stopped.

"JEFF!!!! ARE YOU OUT THERE?!" she screamed toward the front door. Scara had already chambered a shell and the shotgun's muzzle was nearly right up against the door.

There was a sudden, loud pounding on the front door and it was just enough to make Scara squeeze the trigger. She pulled on instinct. The shot put a fist sized hole in the middle of the front door and it blew away the lower half of Ronald Simpkin's face. He wasn't dead when he hit the ground. He was gurgling blood from the hole that used to be his mouth and his eyes were dilating when Scara stepped out and realized exactly what she had done. Jeff came running around from the backyard, the .45 still out in front of him. When he saw his trembling wife with the shotgun by her side, he grabbed it away from her.

"Go call the police. Don't tell them anything. Call them and go wash your hands," Jeff said with a calmness that belied their position.

Scara looked at her husband with muddled eyes and said, "No, you can't. I won't let you."

"Look, just do it. I love you, it's going to be ok, I promise," Jeff said and nodding in assurance. Scara was wiping away tears but she nodded back. Scara turned to go wash her hands and jumped when she heard the shotgun crack again…again…and one last time.

Johnny Pickens was grinning from the other side of the street and whispered, "Serves the bitch right."

———————

Ronald Simpkins knew a lot of people in Augusta. He was fifty six years old when Scara mowed him down on the front porch. She didn't want Jeff to take the fall; she really didn't. He took the shotgun from her and told her to go wash her hands immediately. He tried desperately to calm his wife but Jeff was internally shaken when he saw it was Ronald that Kira gunned down. Ronald was a friend to everybody; he coached recreation league football for Christ's sake. They'd tell the police it was an accident; nothing but a tragic accident; a case of mistaken identity. How could it be mistaken identity when you didn't even ask who was at the door?

The man was in a raincoat and his pajama pants. The man was clearly coming to see if he could help out his neighbor. There was surely something amiss. And for that, he got his face blown off. Now, ain't that a kick in the head? Jeff would take the fall; he would admit to firing the shotgun; albeit in an effort to protect his wife. But, Jeff wouldn't get off scot-free. Jeff would get ten years in prison for voluntary manslaughter, not exactly first degree murder but he wouldn't see Kira for at least five more years if he cut his time in half with model behavior, and that may be a problem because Jeff's temper was very easily provoked. So, Kira would have to move. She would move to Atlanta to be closer to her family. Her mother and sister lived in Decatur so Scara would get an apartment and a job. She would do all of those things. And, even though it was her every intention to cancel the Scotland trip that Jeff had sprang on her during a romantic dinner of burgers less than six months before, she would go and if she had any sort of precursor as to what was coming her way, Scara would have kept her depressed ass at home.

CHAPTER 2

August 4, 2016: 1:30 AM – Augusta, GA

Johnny Pickens was going over the edge of perturbed into furious. He was staring a hole through the restraining order that had been issued to him the day before. The bitch finally did it. She finally took one out on him. Her bedroom light had been out going on three hours now and Johnny had been stewing in his truck for every one of those one hundred eighty minutes; re-reading the restraining order over and over again.

Scara L Moore, Applicant

vs.

John J. Pickens, Adverse Party

Temporary Order of Protection Against Stalking, Aggravated Stalking or Harassment.

YOU, THE ADVERSE PARTY, ARE HEREBY NOTIFIED that ANY INTENTIONAL VIOLATION OF THIS ORDER IS A CRIMINAL VIOLATION and can result in your immediate arrest or issuance of an arrest warrant.

"Adverse party, I'll show that bitch an adverse party. Who the fuck does she think she is?" Johnny was incensed and he was smiling. The time of comeuppance for this horse shit was here. Johnny took a big swallow of the apple pie moonshine he had made for himself and stepped out of his truck.

Scara was lying in the darkness; she could hear the hum of the empty aquarium in her bedroom, the fish had died but the aquarium's hum helped her to sleep on most nights. She almost stayed with her sister because she was nervous about Johnny. Three dates in and the son of a bitch thought he owned her. There were a few signs on their first date, overpowering in conversations, very Johnny-centric, a few too many drinks and almost a forced kiss at the end of the date, an attempt that Scara thankfully avoided. He was just charming enough for her to chalk it up to trying too hard to impress her with machismo on date number one, and when he called the next day she thought, what the hell, let's give it another shot. The second date was better than the first; it was the calm before the torrid storm. He was a gentleman. He held the door open for her. Johnny listened to her and he seemed genuinely interested. And, at the end of date number two, Scara even gave Johnny a gentle peck on the lips. After that, it clicked solid into Johnny's brain that she was now his property. Date three is when all hell broke loose. It was bad from the start. Johnny said that he was taking her somewhere special for dinner. He took her straight to his house. She was hesitant to even get out of his truck but he assured her that he had a nice hot meal waiting for them inside and, according to him; he had spent the better part of two hours cooking and preparing it. She got out and went inside. There was no smell of food in the house. It was a single story home with turd brown shag carpet and a musty smell that seemed to ooze from the walls. Scara turned around almost as soon as they got inside and Johnny blocked the front door. He told her that he was sorry for the, as he called it, little fib, and he had ordered take-out. It would be there in the next fifteen minutes. Scara was a smart woman; she wasn't an easy mark. Johnny pointed toward the well lived in living room and urged her to go sit down on the couch and get comfortable. Scara wasn't sitting or lying down anywhere in that house; she took a few steps toward the living room, acting as if she was going to oblige as she calmly reached into her purse and gripped the keychain sized pepper spray she kept tucked in the front side pocket. Johnny was smiling, he was thinking of where he would have her within an hour and that smile got turned upside down real quick when pepper spray suddenly covered his face and eyes. He shrieked like a frightened ten year old girl as Scara calmly moved around the screeching man and let herself out the door she came in. She didn't call the police, she just walked two blocks over to a convenience store, summoned an Uber, went home and then to bed. She was sure that he had gotten the message. But…he didn't and the phone calls began. At first, she thought he was just testing her to get a reaction, she was no rookie and she simply ignored him. When it didn't stop, she simply blocked his number and then calls started flooding in from multiple numbers. Fucking smart phones and the five hundred million text and phone apps you can download on them. Over the next month, Scara started getting calls at work that was getting her office manager very agitated. Finally, enough was enough and she was granted a temporary restraining order. Scara was notified that it was executed and served.

Johnny took one more drag from his cigarette and raised his leg to kick in the back door. There was a blinding light and the quick chirp of a siren to let him know that two of Augusta's finest had him squarely in their sights. Johnny raised both arms into the air. Scara waited until they had him in the back of the squad car before she stepped outside. She would prosecute and old Johnny Pickens, whose intentions were not pure as the driven snow, would be sentenced to a cool two years in prison. Apparently, this hadn't been Johnny's first run in with the law. Scara was so glad that she spotted his truck across the street when she took a quick peek out of the bedroom window twenty minutes before. It was a damn good thing that she couldn't sleep that night or the outcome may have been much, much more unpleasant, possibly lethal. She did spray him with pepper spray after all and he had to have some sort of feelings about that. Scara would quickly forget about Johnny and meet the love of her life, Jeff Slayfield; two weeks after Johnny went off to the pokey.

CHAPTER 3

August 8, 2018: 12:00 PM – Augusta, GA

Serving almost two years in prison gave Johnny plenty of time to reflect on his mistakes. He wasn't very pleased to find out that the lady that put him there had just gotten married. He wasn't happy that Scara was able to put him out of her memory so quickly. He'd have to remind her of lost love. He had scoped out Jeff Slayfield on Facebook. He was certainly a big boy and not someone that Johnny wanted to face straight up, man to man. That would not be very smart of old Johnny Pickens and even though he wasn't very bright in the sense that he telegraphed every move before with Scara, he was bright in the sense that he had learned from that mistake. He'd be stealthy this go around. He'd get Jeff out of the picture and swoop in to claim what was his. That's how this shit was going to work.

Burner phones, check, text apps, check, Facebook connections to Scara's friends and family, check. It was easy-peasy to get her number and even easier to get her address. Modern technology was such a wonderful thing. It gives access to so much information for the lazy stalker to find his prey and push the start button on Operation Scara. This game would be fun.

"Let's check out Scara's Facebook page," Johnny smiled as it loaded on his phone. Of course, Johnny Pickens was blocked but her old friend, Alayna Marie's Facebook page had been inactive for a while and she blindly accepted a new friend request from the fake page Johnny created. Smart phones are a stalker's best friend.

"You and Jeff are happily married, huh?" Johnny picked at his teeth with the cleaner end of a blunt tooth pick. "Guess we'll just see about that."

Jeff and Scara were married four months before Johnny got out of prison. He took her on a seven day Bahamas cruise. "What a cheap fuck," Johnny whispered. Johnny clicked on the Google Maps icon on his Android phone and typed the address, 235 Woodlawn Drive, Augusta GA. The phone reached out to cyberspace and was pondering Johnny's request before it came back with an image labeled street view. Johnny clicked on the image and was impressed by the eighteen hundred square foot home that filled the front of his screen. He magically moved the view with the swipe of his finger and he could see that the house was on a nice sized piece of property with a fenced in backyard. It was going to be almost too easy.

The Book Tavern – Augusta, GA

Scara was perusing the books in the travel section of the beloved downtown bookstore. She was looking for anything related to Scottish lore. It had always been a dream of hers and her late brother, Joey, to take a trip to Scotland. Scara loved coming into this store. She made an appearance at least twice a week just to get a whiff of that "old book" smell in this neatly kept shop.

David Hutchison was the owner of this establishment and he looked as if he could have played in the NBA in another life. He stood all of six feet six and had a slender frame that would have been perfect for rebounding and three point jumpers. He had a long brown beard that matched the short hair on top of his head. David was a book lover and huge supporter of the local artist and author scene; often hosting author signings and art events specifically for the homegrown talent. And he didn't mind when Scara came into his store even if she didn't buy anything; which wasn't very often. She was great to talk to and not bad to look at. David saw her searching as he approached, smiling and waving.

"Hey, Scara, can I help you find something in particular?"

"David, hey...I'm looking for something about Scotland? Do you have any sorts of books on Scotland's mythology?"

David scratched at his beard and his smile got wider. Scara was expecting good news based upon the look and she wasn't disappointed.

"It's funny you mentioned Scottish mythology. A lady turned in a book just last week on that very topic. Come with me."

Scara grinned and followed behind David as they moved toward the check out counter.

"I think I still have it in the stack in the back. I haven't gotten around to putting one of our labels on it yet."

Scara waited as David stepped into the small check in area that was located right beside the front counter. A couple of minutes had gone by when he emerged with a hefty book in his hand.

"Here it is, *The Lore of Scotland, A Guide To Scottish Legends*," he said and handed it over to Scara.

"Oh David, thank you so much, this is perfect," Scara said as she happily ogled the colorful cover. It was covered in castle illustrations. "How much?" was her follow up question.

"Well, I was going to put a ten dollar sticker on it but for you I'll make it a seven dollar sticker," David said.

Scara handed over a ten dollar bill and said, "Keep the change." David smiled.

"Thank you, Scara. I know you read King sometimes. A lady called me earlier and said she'd be turning in a copy of *The Outsider*. I'll hold it if you're interested."

"Maybe another time, thank you for telling me though. Stephen King already has a shit ton of my money," Scara said and patted the book she just bought.

David chuckled. "Yeah, he does have a shit ton of money and so do his kids riding the coat tails of daddy's name as they write their drivel." David obviously wasn't a fan of the kiddie Kings' work.

"*In The Tall Grass* wasn't that bad, I rather enjoyed it, the movie sucked but the book was pretty good," Scara replied.

"Didn't the elder King help out with that one?"

"Well, yeah, he did. Gotta' go, David. I'll see you next week."

"See you next week, Scara."

Scara could hardly wait to get home so she could crack open her new treasure. She wished Joey were here to read it with her.

The setup in the Book Tavern is such that when you walk into the store, most of the new titles and more popular used titles cover a large portion of the lower level which sensibly takes up most of the floor space. There is a staircase off to the left when you walk in the front door that leads up to a room that houses more unique reading selections along with a few harder to find DVD movies and LPs. The man couldn't hold back his grin as he was flipping through the LPs. He couldn't care less who the bands were as he mindlessly filed through record after record. His attention was fully on the buxom black haired woman speaking with David on the lower level. She had his complete and undivided attention. He grinned when David emerged with a thick book in his hand. The man stopped with the records and whispered to himself, "Scara, you'll be kissing me again very soon and you are going to love me again." Johnny Pickens waited until he heard the bell of the exit before he moved quickly downstairs to follow the bitch that had him locked up.

Scara hopped into her Kia Sorento and pulled out of the parking spot. Johnny waited for her to leave completely before he cranked his worse for wear Suzuki motorcycle. It belched exhaust as he pulled off to follow the Sorento down the street. *Over the hills and through the woods to grandma's house we go*, repeated in his mind. He was going to make sure he got the house right when he Googled it and what better way to make absolutely sure than to follow the bitch home.

Jeff was waiting for her when she got home.

"Where's Sheena?" were Scara's first words when she walked into the door holding up her new book.

"She's in the backyard killing something. I see you found another one, huh? What is your obsession with Scotland anyway?"

"Reminds me of good times with my brother, that's all. We were supposed to go together."

Jeff nodded his head and dropped the Scotland subject.

"I think we should go grab a bite, not mess with the kitchen or pots or pans or anything like that," Scara said and set the book on the coffee table.

"So, go to *Five Guys* when we have a shit ton of food in the fridge? Makes perfect sense to me," Jeff grinned his smart ass grin. Scara grinned back and flipped the middle finger.

"Look, I want *Five Guys*, smartass, and you're going to pay for it and you're going to like it."

"*Five Guys*, that don't sound so bad, I could use a good burger and fries. Ok, you convinced me."

"Well, go get ready," Scara said as she walked to the kitchen. She was going to let Sheena in before they left the house.

"Alright, Kira, ready to roll."

"You're not wearing sweatpants to Five Guys, go put on some pants."

"Ugh, nobody gives a shit," Jeff replied.

"Yeah, somebody gives a shit and that somebody is me. You can leave on the t-shirt but put on some jeans. There is at least five pair in your closet."

"Yes, ma'am," Jeff jumped from his chair and gave a three fingered salute.

"That's more like it. Now, move your ass. Mama is hungry. Sheena! Come on, girl!"

Scara could hear the cat rustling around the back of the shed and she didn't want to walk all the way across the yard so she grabbed a treat bag and started shaking it vigorously. A lightning fast ball of brown and white fur tore from the shed, up the back deck and slid into the kitchen as if she were rounding third and getting to home plate.

"Good girl," Scara said and poured a handful of treats onto the tiled floor. Sheena had the pieces scarfed up and begging for more.

"I'll give you more when we get home, go lay down in your spot," Scara said as she gave Sheena a quick pet.

"You ready to roll, babe?" Jeff came down the hallway with real pants on.

"I am now." She grabbed her man's hand and they walked out the front door.

———

Johnny watched as the happy couple emerged from the house. He saw the big man locking the front door and Scara half jogging to the big Chevy pickup (definitely suited for a man Jeff's size). He'd wait a good ten minutes after they were gone before he would get off of his bike and stroll towards the house. He needed a closer look. There was no house to the right of the Slayfield's but about fifty yards to the left was a neat little home, couldn't have been more than twelve hundred square feet and as Johnny stepped off of the bike, he saw a thin man exit the front door holding a leash. Attached to the leash was a small dog of some kind, Johnny wasn't really up on dog species but he moved to the side of his bike and pretended he was looking for something in the saddlebags. The man didn't seem to pay Johnny any mind as he moved quickly to keep pace with the little dog that was urging him along for a walk; a walk that seemed very familiar to both of them. Johnny let them get far enough away before he moved toward the Slayfield house. First, he examined the front of the house. It was a straight away entry with no fenced in front yard. He could walk directly up onto the front porch if he wanted. Johnny was thinking that it probably had one of those fancy doorbells equipped with a camera so he was careful not to actually walk into the driveway. Johnny kept his distance as he made his way past the front of the house and his eyes roamed to the area that was fenced in; the side and backyard had a chain link fence that ran all the way around the back of the house and married up to their neighbor's on the left. The backyard was much larger than the front; a solid acre and was full of trees. Johnny didn't know it but they were pecan trees. The pecan trees housed squirrels by the hundreds; squirrels that kept Sheena active when she was let out to roam around. Johnny also noticed the shed that was set about fifteen yards or so behind the house. The lawn was plush and full. Johnny was sure that there was some sweet riding lawn mower being housed in the big shed out back.

"Well, she got what she wanted. She got her man. She got the nice house and the big backyard. Good for her," Johnny mumbled to himself as he walked back to the motorcycle. He'd catch up with her and her new man in a bit. Johnny briefly thought about hanging around and speaking with the neighbor when he got back from walking the dog but dismissed it. He might come back when he had a little more time. He needed to get going to Wal-Mart to speak to a certain department manager and find out if he had secured a job for him or not.

Five Guys

"I love these burgers," Jeff said as he picked up the double cheeseburger with everything.

"I know, they are so good," Scara agreed as she took a bite of her own. She liked hers with ketchup, mustard and pickles; not with all of the, as she called it, yucky stuff that Jeff preferred.

"Kira, listen I want to talk to you about something," Jeff said and set the burger down. His tone was suddenly solemn so Scara thought he was fucking with her.

"Ok, Mr. Serious, what do you want to talk about?"

"Well, it's about the cruise we went on. You enjoyed it didn't you?"

"You know that I did."

"Are you sure? We got a great deal on it, don't get me wrong and the water was so blue and everything was so perfect. There was no place in the world that I would have rather been with you," Jeff mugged as he lifted the sandwich back to his face. The words rang true but he had that grin on his face that only came out when he was fucking with her.

"Where are you going with this? I loved every minute of it. Are you taking me on another cruise? I will blow you right now if you say that you are."

"Whoa, whoa, this is a family restaurant and I'm not taking you on another cruise but after that offer I think maybe I should have," he said and then dipped a fry in ketchup.

"What did you do?" Scara asked with her own grin spreading under her nose.

"Nothing."

"Bullshit, you did something."

"Who, me? Would I do anything?"

"Yes."

"Wait here for a minute," Jeff said as he dabbed a napkin to his lips and chin, "I'll be right back so don't touch my food."

"Where are you going?"

"To the truck real quick, be right back."

"What the fuck has he done?" Scara whispered to herself. She was getting butterflies in her stomach. It was almost as if she were expecting Jeff to ask her to marry him all over again. He had neatly folded papers in his hand when he walked back into the restaurant.

"Ok," Jeff started and set the papers in the seat beside him, "let me take another bite of this burger first."

"Asshole," Scara said and shook her head. The suspense was killing her but she was trying not to give him the satisfaction; she was failing.

"Ok, damn that's a good burger, maybe I should take another..."

"Jeff, what the fuck?!"

"Ok, ok. Look, I've been thinking a lot about that honeymoon and it was great. It really was."

"But..." Scara interrupted.

"But, but, but you got me Kira. I just don't think it quite measured up to what you deserved. I just happen to know of a place that you have wanted to visit ever since you were just a wee hen."

Scara's eyes were welling up. "You didn't."

Jeff was taking another bite of his burger and was shaking his head up and down.

"Those papers aren't what I think they are?"

"If they are, you remember what you said if they were cruise tickets? I can't wait to see what you're going to do for this," Jeff opened the papers and handed them over to Scara. They were plane ticket reservations with the destination Edinburgh, Scotland. There was also a booking itinerary for the High Street hotel. These were good for August the following year. That would be enough time to acquire passports and get everything lined up. Scara was trembling.

She had always wanted to go. Scara and her late brother Joey talked about it constantly growing up. Which immediately brought another question to mind, how could they afford such a trip?

"Oh my God, Jeff. This is too much. We can't...I mean how can we? This better not be a joke or I will divorce your ass."

"The money? Don't worry about that, I have it all taken care of and don't worry, I didn't go into debt to do it, I promise."

"Then how?" Scara pressed, but not too hard. She was staring at the beautiful images from the High Street hotel already pulled up on her phone.

"Don't worry about how, I have it covered and we will be headed to Queensferry when we get there."

"I don't know what to say. I'm speechless."

"Well back to that blowing thing."

"Shut up, just wait until we get home," she replied.

Jeff took another big bite from his burger. "Well whatever we do, we need to wait a little bit for this burger to settle."

"I love you, jackass," Scara said to her husband.

"I love you too, Kira, I'd take a bullet for you," Jeff replied. He didn't know how close to the truth that would turn out to be. He'd take the slap from the long hand of the law so that she could remain free. But, nothing is ever free.

CHAPTER 4

August 10, 2018: 10:30 PM – Augusta, GA

Johnny got the job. He wasn't super thrilled about it. He wasn't all that jazzed about stocking pet supplies at the local Wal-Mart but it was a means to an end. He volunteered for the overnight shift which made him an even more attractive hire. If there was one thing true in the Deep South, more of the people were early to bed and early to rise than vice versa so there was more demand for night shift positions than day. It wasn't so bad for Johnny, he wasn't much of a sleeper anyway; he was a four to five hour a night kind of guy. That would give him a lot of time to focus on his plan to win Scara back.

It was his first night stocking shelves for Wally World and he was efficient in handling pet supplies. He had the pallets of kitty litter and dog food all pulled out and shelved in half the time of his predecessor - which was not the reason his predecessor was let go, that was for trying to load a 65" Samsung Smart-TV into the back of his pickup one late night. Johnny surprised himself at how quickly he got everything out; he'd be sure to pace himself the next night. It would actually be rather shocking for him to see how much pet food and cat litter was purchased in one average day at America's Favorite Fun Park, Wally World. Johnny made his way over to electronics to have a gander at what was new in Wal-Mart technology land.

"Sweet Jesus," he muttered. He found himself looking at the Logistimatics Mobile - 200 GPS Tracker with Live Audio Monitoring. It was a stalker's dream; small enough to hide easily in or on a vehicle. Johnny was startled out of his technology trance.

"Hey, I'm Kevin," said the slender kid with shaggy blonde hair as he extended his hand for a shake.

"Hey, I see that," Johnny replied as he grabbed the kid's dainty hand with a more than firm grip, "it's on your name badge, just like me, and you see I'm John but you can call me Johnny."

"Hey, Johnny," Kevin's smile receded a little as he moved his hand back and forth; Johnny's grip wasn't what he expected in a first greeting hand shake. Millenials were just soft turds – that was Johnny's line of thinking when it came to fresh faced kids like Kevin. "That's new; we just got a few of them yesterday."

"You don't say?" Johnny replied. "You work the electronics section, do you?"

"Yes sir, guilty as charged!" Kevin threw up his hands and flashed the whitest smile Johnny had ever seen. Johnny was thinking, *fruit loop*, but just smiled back at the goofy looking fuck in front of him.

"So, this thing works with a smart phone, huh? You got a key to this case; I might want to buy one of these."

"What for?"

"It's for a project. Project Nunya," Johnny answered.

"Project Nunya? Sounds interesting, what's that?" Kevin asked in all seriousness.

Millenials can't be this fucking stupid is what Johnny thought when he replied, "Well, it's a very special project, Kevin."

"Why is it called Project Nunya? That somebody's name?"

This fucker is absolutely clueless Johnny thought but kept a straight face. "No, it's not somebody's name. Nunya is code, Kevin. A special code. You gonna' open this case for me or are we waiting until the day shift gets here?" Johnny asked, knowing all well that dumb-ass Kevin here was going to keep pushing and he didn't disappoint.

"Ok, I'll open it but first you have to tell me what Nunya is code for."

"Ok, I will but you need to come closer. I don't want to just blurt it out. You know Sam Walton's ghost may be around listening."

"Who's Sam Walton?"

This motherfucker has to be kidding me, Johnny thought. They talked about Sam Walton repeatedly during employee orientation. His grinning old bird face is on the handbook. Apparently millennial Kevin was smoking some good shit on his first day. "It doesn't matter. You want to know the Nunya code, right?"

"I do," Kevin whispered back. He was going to be part of a big secret with Johnny. Project Nunya had to be awesome as fuck.

"Come closer, I have to whisper the Nunya code in your ear."

Kevin leaned close to Johnny – Kevin was a tall kid – and Johnny moved close to Kevin's ear and whispered.

"Ok, Nunya means....nun...ya....fuckin...business," Johnny finished his menacing whisper and backed away from Kevin. Kevin's face turned red and he fumbled for the key to the case.

"If you didn't want me to ...."

"Shhhhhhh..... I said don't tell nobody, Kevin. You're the only one other than me with the Nunya code so don't dilly dally; I want to read the box. Don't make me kill you and take the keys," Johnny said in a way that let Kevin know to stay out of his fucking way and don't ask him any more fucking questions. Johnny did it with a smile that would make the late great Sam Walton very proud. Kevin opened the case and Johnny grabbed the box.

"You can leave now, Kevin, I promise I'll lock it back up or buy it. One or the other, I'll let you know."

Kevin slunk away and took a couple of quick glances back to Johnny as he did so.

"Now, this thing," Johnny was talking to himself – there wasn't a lot of people in the store after 2 AM. "I have to have an Android or Apple phone. Ok, my Samsung is an Android so we're good there. I download an app, sure I'll need an email address to register the fucking thing," Johnny said as if he were really having a conversation with someone. "Good thing Mark Johnson from Savannah, GA has a new email address and phone number," Johnny whispered. He admired his own stealth, what better fake name to use on a Microsoft Hotmail account than Mark Johnson? "I know where the bitch lives, check. I know which car the bitch drives, check. Time to get acquainted with her driving habits,"

Johnny finished his solo conversation. "Oh, Kevin! I'd like to make a purchase!"

August 11, 2018: 7:45 AM

Scara woke up fresh and happy. She could hear Jeff milling around in the kitchen and Sheena was curled up in a furry white and brown ball at the foot of the bed. Scara couldn't believe this was her life. She was afraid to pinch herself; afraid if she did that she would wake up from a coma in a hospital somewhere. If this world wasn't real, it was real enough to her and she would much rather live here than die in the other place.

Scara let the thoughts of silence escape her mind as quickly as they had scurried in; they were going to Scotland. Next August, they would be in Scotland enjoying the sights and sounds of Edinburgh and South Queensferry.

"Morning, Kira," Jeff said as he smiled at his wife. He thought she was at her most beautiful first thing in the morning before any make up covered her natural features. The first thing that attracted Jeff to her was Kira's high cheek bones. Many a model would scratch eyes to have such cheek bones. Her hair was naturally brunette but she made sure that it was always black as night. The second thing that really sealed the deal of attraction for Jeff was Kira's smile. A smile that lights up a room is a cliché old as time but like he said about the song from the movie she loathed, just because it's been said a million times didn't mean it wasn't true.

"Hey sexy man," Scara bared her teeth and Jeff pointed toward the coffee pot. "It's ready, babe. Pour yourself a cup."

"Yes, sir, Mr. Slayfield, how about some music?" Scara asked as she turned her direction to the Google mini sitting on the kitchen counter.

"You know that's how they track us, Kira," Jeff said.

"Shut up, Google play ZZ Ward," Scara said in the device's direction. And it immediately boomed with ZZ's latest, *Sex and Stardust.*

"Hey, it's a new one," Scara said happily as she raised the cup of coffee to her lips.

"Yeah, it sounds pretty good," Jeff responded. He pointed to the bar. "Grab a stool, my dear." Jeff set the plate of sunny side up eggs and turkey bacon with slightly burnt toast down in front of his smiling wife.

"You know where my heart is, don't you?"

"I thought you might want to sleep in. I was actually going to serve you this in bed but you messed up the works by coming in here."

"I smelled the bacon; the real bacon." Scara pointed at the pork bacon sitting on Jeff's plate.

"You're the one that wanted this turkey crap so if that's what you want, that's what you get." Jeff smiled and put a slice of the real stuff in between his teeth.

"Jackass," Scara replied and spread the grape jelly on her purposely burnt toast – that's just the way she liked it. "I'm excited about our trip. You think you want to tell me about the surprise you have in store when we get there? You really think you're gonna' keep that secret until we get there?"

"I'm gonna' give it the old college try. Listen, I've got to go to work for a few hours today and tonight we can go catch a movie if you want. You can even invite what's her face and her husband, what's his name, Mike or something?" Jeff asked smart-assedly, already knowing the answer – Vicky and Josh were the pair and they lived in the neighborhood. Scara made friends with Vicky while jogging around their neighborhood less than a week after moving into their home.

"Yeah, I'll give what's her name and Mike or something a call in a little while. But, instead of a movie, I want to go to a concert. They would be right up your alley."

"Look, I know you love Garbage but I'm not that big of a fan even though the red head is smoking." Jeff reached for his wife's hand and she slapped it.

"If it were Garbage, I wouldn't be asking. I know you would want to go to this show. I'm not even going to tell you who it is now. I want to have a surprise of my own," Scara said, thinking you're not the only one with surprises.

"Hey Google, who is playing music in Augusta tonight?"

Scara's jaw dropped at her husband's craftiness.

"The Casket Creatures are playing at The James Brown Arena at 7:30 PM. Night Train is playin..."

"Hey Google, stop. See, I kind of like that thing now."

"You are such an asshole, no fun bitch."

"That ain't what you said last night," Jeff shot back. "Let me get on to work so I can get back here and get my face paint on. Casket Creatures!!!! Hell YEAH!!!!!"

"I'll get the tickets and I'll message one of the boys to let them know we'll be there. Now, carry your asshole self to work, please," Scara said as she reached over the bar and pulled a slice of bacon from Jeff's plate.

Jeff kissed his wife and left the house. Sheena made her way down the hallway after she heard front door close, meowing to her heart's content.

"You didn't want to see Daddy this morning? You want some of this?" Scara held the turkey bacon toward the floor and Sheena sniffed the air and kept walking toward her food bowl. Even she wasn't a fan of the fake bacon.

Johnny watched the red dot stay stationary on the app for the Logistimatics Mobile - 200 GPS Tracker. Her Kia Sorento was still parked in the driveway. The app would alert him when Scara was on the move. Jeff once again marveled at how easy modern technology was making this for him. He didn't have to report to Wal-Mart until later that night so he had some time to kill. He fired up The Facebook to see what was going on in Scara's virtual world and as soon as her profile page loaded, Johnny grinned. Scara's latest Facebook update was a picture of her kissing Jeff with the caption:

Jeff is whisking me away to Scotland next summer. If I'm not the luckiest girl in the world, I don't know who is.

Johnny picked at his teeth as he read the caption and gave it a thought, *maybe he's not the man you think he is, Scara.* Just as Johnny finished his thought, the app dinged and let him know that Scara was on the move. He'd just watch the red dot and see where she ended up.

CHAPTER 5

August 13, 2018: 3:00 PM – Augusta, GA

Scara felt something tickle her brain. She couldn't explain it but something wasn't quite right. She was almost to the cemetery. She hadn't paid her brother a visit in well over a year and what would have been his twenty eighth birthday was fast approaching. His death was a quiet one – a last breath on a cold night in his warm bed. Joey suffered from an undetected hole in his heart and he went into cardiac arrest while he dreamt of flying into space. Joey kept floating skyward and he never felt the cold; never felt any pain; never felt the sting of the reaper. He died as peacefully as a human being could ever hope to die, no matter the age. He died in the silence.

Scara was closer to Joey than her mother or sister. Joey was Scara's confidant. She'd tell him things she would never dream of telling anyone else. She told him about the first boy she did it with and how unremarkable it really was. Scara smiled as she remembered Joey giggling and telling her that she should have saved herself for her one true love.

Scara had known it well before Joey told her but she was the first one he came out of the closet to. Joey could tell as soon as it escaped his lips that it wasn't news to his big sister and this made him love her even more. Joey was Betty to Scara's Veronica. He had blonde hair and ocean blue eyes. He was a beautiful human and would make woman and man alike stop in their tracks when he passed by.

The morning he died, Scara felt it. She didn't know how she felt it but she did. It was almost like the stories of twins that say that they can sense the others feelings or knows when the other is in some sort of trouble. She called his cell phone and it rang enough for her to know that it didn't go straight to voice mail, which it would do if he rejected the call, but he would never reject Scara's call. She knew some bad shit was happening and she caught the attention of the state patrol when she floored it to get to Joey's apartment. She didn't give a shit about the blue lights flashing behind her. Everything was moving in slow motion and fast as a blur at the same time. Scara darted from her car with a policeman screaming to **STOP!** She didn't give a shit. He would have to shoot her to keep her from sprinting to Apartment 138. Scara had the key in her hand and the policeman was closing in behind her. She slid the key into the bottom lock with a precision that was scary and pushed the door open and was in her brother's bedroom in an eye blink. She remembered feeling Joey's face. It was so cold. The policeman holstered his weapon as soon as he walked into the room. He immediately realized what was happening and just stood in the doorway until Scara turned to him.

"I'll never get to talk to him again," was all she could say.

The memories hit her every time she visited the cemetery and she figured that played into why she hadn't been here in a while. She felt shame when she approached the tombstone. There hadn't been fresh flowers in the empty vase for a long time and she hadn't brought any. The grave was lonely and forgotten and this sent Scara into a sobbing fit. She was a terrible sister. Her brother deserved better than this. He called her every day he lived and she couldn't sit with him in over a year; how dreadful of a person would do such a thing. This is what Scara thought of herself. She sat, Indian style, directly in front of the tombstone.

"Hey Joey, it's me!" Scara tried to sound cheerful but her voice had the hiccup of a fresh cry.

"I'm sorry that I haven't been here in a while. I want to lie and say that I've been so busy or that things have been so hectic but a year...I know, that's pretty shitty and I am sorry. So, here's the thing, I'm married now and you would have loved him. His name is Jeff, Jeff Slayfield. He took me to the Bahamas for our honeymoon and you won't believe what he just told me. You remember where you and I used to talk about going all the time? Yes, Joey, he's taking me to Scotland. Edinburgh to be exact and I still can't believe that I'm actually going. I just wish you were going with me. Mom and Lisa are doing fine, I'm sure they've both been out here since you've seen me last. Joey, I'm sure the reason I haven't been here in so long is that I was afraid, afraid to sit here at this tombstone again, afraid to laugh in the open air having a one way discussion with a cold piece of granite. I want to believe you can hear me. I want to believe you are watching from above and smiling at me right now. I really want to believe these things with all of my heart. But, the difference in what I want to believe and the reality of my true feelings are quite a stretch from one to the other. What I really think is I'm just talking to a rock while what's left of you has decayed under the rock. I want to tell you that I'll come visit you more often. I felt that I had to come and get all of this off of my chest. The void left without you in my life will never be filled. And now, I'm rambling on just like one of those fucking Hallmark movies. I don't know why I had to come out...well, that's not exactly true. This is my proper goodbye and even though your ears won't hear it, mine will. I won't come back here. I'm going to live my life like you wanted me to. I love you, brother. I'll join you in the silence one day."

The grin spread across Johnny's face. He was seated and leaning against Lisa Kane's large tombstone. He heard every word of Scara's confession of non-belief. Silence is where she would go. Silence is where she would face her final stop. Johnny didn't want that; he just wanted her to see things his way. He stayed put until the crunch of the ground as Scara walked away was completely gone and, even then, he waited until he saw the little red dot moving on his screen before he got to his feet.

CHAPTER 6

August, 20, 2018: 2:15 AM – Augusta, GA

It was time to fuck up Scara's life now. It was late and it was raining. He had taken the night off from Wal-Mart for this momentous occasion. Johnny was dressed in black sweats with a matching hoodie. He could hear the rain coming down in a steady pattern. He was going to pay Scara and her husband an early morning visit.

Johnny was thinking about the affectionate display he witnessed between the two just hours before. It was just about time to go make Mrs. Slayfield a widow. They would be fast asleep by now. Scara would regret the day she fucked over Johnny Pickens. The GPS tracker had done its job; Johnny observed Scara's travel patterns for a couple of weeks and there was nothing in those patterns that jumped out to Johnny. He pulled the hoodie over the top of his already wet head. It was a cold rain and it slapped at Johnny's face in a steady cadence; not too hard but enough to keep him focused on the task at hand. Johnny walked past the front of the house and took a left turn where the backyard fence line began. His heart was racing. He wasn't going to get caught the same way twice. The only motion sensors were the ones at the front of the home; the back was dark. Johnny had seen Jeff pull up on the fence latch and push. To someone that didn't know how to do it, the fence wouldn't budge, it would appear to be locked tight but Johnny knew the trick because he had seen Jeff do it at least four or five times now…simple enough. He gripped the hunting knife by its stark aluminum handle. He wanted to make this kill up close and personal. The wet leaves were slick and Johnny was mindful of them as he approached the back deck. He could feel the excitement building. It was better than the slow build up of a good lay. The wind picked up just a bit and Johnny grinned when he saw what he recognized as the light from a refrigerator through the dark window. It was her. Scara was right there. He could make out her long black hair as it caught a glimmer from the light of the fridge. Johnny pulled the knife close to his face before he placed the point directly onto the kitchen window and ran it across the pane. Scara moved away from the kitchen as if she were checking something real quick. Johnny didn't know it was Sheena that she was checking on to make sure that the cat hadn't been left outside. Johnny pulled the knife across the window again, more aggressively this time and he could see Scara's figure moving toward the kitchen window. Johnny scampered down the back porch steps, again careful of the slick leaves when his sneakers touched the ground. He receded into the darkness when Scara switched on the deck lights. The next thing he heard was her screaming right before he ducked into the shed. He'd ambush dear hubby when he came to check out what Scara was screaming about. He'd plunge that hunting knife deep into the soft flesh of Jeff's neck. He'd be out of there after the fatal stick and Scara could watch her man bleed out in front of her and there wouldn't be a damned thing that she could do about it.

Johnny was damn near salivating when he heard Jeff bellowing from the back porch. He ran out into the rain in only his boxers and he was armed. Johnny did let the thought that maybe he just fucked up creep into his mind but he hunkered down and made himself small. Jeff would be inside the shed in a matter of seconds and he'd only have one shot at this. He'd have to stick him quickly and deeply before he made his get away.

Jeff wasn't fucking around. If it was who Scara thought it was, he was going to blow his fucking head off. Jeff stopped short of the shed and steadied his breath. He was listening; trying to hear through the rain; trying to hear any sound of someone else within earshot; heavy breathing of a nervous would be predator that was just now realizing that he was prey. All he could hear was the rain. Jeff pulled the shed door open. Johnny was tensing up inside, his knuckles were white as he tightened his grip on the handle. The blood was almost completely gone from his fingers. His lips quivered just a bit. Johnny saw the bare skin of Jeff's torso as he stepped into the shed. He only needed to take a few steps; just a few and he would open the blood spigot. Johnny was coiled like a rattlesnake; poised for the strike; needing the strike. He could taste the satisfaction of removing happiness from Scara's life just as she had done to him. Jeff took another step and Johnny began to slowly rise, the rhythm of the rain seemed to egg him on.

KABOOM!!!!!!!

And just like that, Jeff was gone. He scampered out of the shed and was already around the fence, running to the front of the house.

"What the fuck just happened?" Johnny whispered as he walked out of the shed. He stood there not knowing how to feel for another minute before he heard more shotgun blasts. He moved quickly back the way he came and let himself out. Johnny pulled the hoodie from his head as he ran across the street and into wooded cover. He moved around to get a distant look at the front porch. And, boy oh boy, what did he see but a man lying face up in a pool of blood with Mr. Slayfield holding a shotgun that he didn't have just a few moments before. This was working out even better than Johnny had hoped and he didn't even have to kill the fucker. Now, that did disappoint him just a little. It was time to sit back and see how this shit would play out. He'd see to it that Scara wouldn't stay lonely very long.

Three weeks later.

Scara knew it was Johnny. She caught a glimpse of him in the backyard but it was nothing that she could prove. Scara had once told Jeff her almost horror story of one Johnny Pickens and the night her bladder thankfully didn't let her sleep. She remembered Jeff saying, "If he comes around again, you won't need a restraining order," and that was all the assurance that Scara needed at the time.

Jeff's attorney was submitting the plea deal that would get him ten years instead of twenty or more and Scara was worried about

Johnny Pickens. She was positive that it was him in their backyard and incorrectly assumed that he set up poor Mr. Ronald Simpkins somehow. As it turned out, it was just blind luck in Johnny's favor and misfortune for Mr. Simpkins. She hadn't heard a peep from Johnny since she mowed down Mr. Simpkins. Of course, she hadn't slept very much since Jeff was taken away. Her mother and sister offered to come keep her company but she told them to stay away; again, not knowing what fucked up thing Johnny may do next. She thought about going to Atlanta to be closer to them but she couldn't leave Jeff; not yet. Not until the judge passed final sentence and then there would be no reason for her to stay in Augusta. The drive was close enough that she could visit and she would, a lot, at first. Scara also had a few loose ends to tie up before she moved to the ATL.

It was a Saturday morning and she was going to venture out to the grocery store that morning. Sheena was watching from her perch in the window. Scara looked back at her cat with her first real smile in three weeks. Scara reached for the car door handle and stopped when she heard a chirp; a chirp that sounded almost like a smoke detector when the battery was about to give up the ghost. She waited a few seconds and there was another chirp; it was very close.

"What the hell?" Scara walked to the back of her Sorento and listened for the next chirp and it came. Sheena was still watching curiously from the window. Scara leaned under the back bumper; her long hair was touching the concrete. She observed a small, red blinking light. Scara reached for it but it was just out of her grasp; someone with longer arms put it there. She stood up and took a quick look around to make sure that the person that put it there wasn't making a bee line for her right now. Once she was satisfied that wasn't the case, Scara lay flat on her back on the driveway, looking like a backyard mechanic, and slid under the bumper far enough for her to reach the device. She heard the ripping sound of Velcro separating when she tugged on it and secured it in her palm. The back of the device had the words Logistimatics Mobile 200 etched into the black plastic molding. The device chirped again and Scara was sure that it was running low on juice. She flipped it over. It looked as if a standard micro USB charger would resuscitate it and she was pretty sure who put it there. Scara thought about taking it into the house and letting it charge while she was out but she didn't want her visitor to show and know the jig was up. She wanted to keep this rabbit in the hole a little longer. Now that she knew it was there, she could use it to her advantage. She plugged it into the car charger and when the engine sprung to life the device stopped chirping and the red flashing light turned amber to indicate that the device was charging. Johnny must have been able to turn this thing on and off remotely with a phone app is what Scara figured. He must have forgotten to turn it off for a while. Well, if Johnny wanted to see where she was going, she'd let him.

Wal-Mart

The app dinged to life as Johnny schlepped dog food from the stock room. Scara was on the move. Johnny pulled the phone from his pocket. Kevin walked by at that moment but didn't give Johnny a second look. He wanted no part of Project Nunya or anything to do with one Johnny Pickens.

Johnny decided it was break time and moved quickly through the store and stepped outside where he lit up a Newport and watched the red dot.

"You gotta' be shitting me," he giggled to himself as the red dot tracked closer and closer to his location. She was coming right to him. "Welcome to Wal-Mart, Scara, where all of your dreams can come true," Johnny said aloud and he got a curious look from an elderly woman to whom he turned and asked, "Is your name Scara, old lady? I didn't think so. The prune juice is on aisle nine. Thank you for shopping at Wal-Mart."

Johnny took a slightly extended, *on the clock*, break until he saw Scara's Sorento whisk into the parking lot. Johnny took one last, long drag from his cigarette before flicking it to the sidewalk to let it finish burning out.

Scara got out of the car and was hit with a quick gust of wind which blew her hair in all kinds of crazy directions. She reached into her purse and pulled out a black hair band and worked her hair through it as she walked rapidly through the parking lot to the welcoming double doors of America's favorite retailer. Scara mindlessly pulled on the first cart in the bay and it wouldn't budge. She tugged on the next one with the same result.

"Let me help you with that, ma'am," she heard the man say as he stepped beside her and gripped the cart handle firmly with both hands.

"What the fuck?" Scara asked. Johnny was standing there grinning at her. Grinning like he just won the state lottery.

"Welcome to Wal-Mart," Johnny replied as he gave the cart a hard and fast tug. It was freed from its grip on the cart behind it.

"Fuck you," Scara said. She, surprisingly, didn't feel fear. Her anger overrode any emotion that may have been festering in that moment. "So, this is where you're working? I know you were behind that shit."

"To what shit are your referring? I'm on the straight and narrow now. I don't want no more trouble with Johnny Law."

"You think you're so fucking smart, Johnny!" Scara was fast approaching full rage. "You're nowhere near as smart as you think and probably twice as fucking stupid as I think you are and that's pretty fucking stupid. My advice to you is to stay the fuck away from me or I swear to God, you won't have to worry about Johnny Law," Scara finished and angrily snatched the cart from his hands. She wasn't going to give him the satisfaction of showing him that he made her leave. She'd do her shopping and carry her ass back home. She had an unknown advantage now. Old Johnny didn't know that she knew that he was tracking her and that was a great thing. Scara actually cracked a tiny little smile as she pushed her cart to the Produce section and thought he thinks he's a fucking mastermind but he's nothing but a masturbator with a pea brain.

Scara's apparent lack of fear excited Johnny. He'd put the fear into her and he was going to really enjoy the conversion. He thought about taking a quick jaunt to the parking lot to take a peek under the Sorento but decided against it. He didn't need Scara coming back out while he was dicking around her car. She may actually be able to take action on that. He'd go see her at his leisure.

One week later.

Scara had studied the tracking device a little more and perused a few message boards dedicated to this sort of technology. She learned that there was a *developer* mode which she could access from the device itself without the need for the smart phone application. There was a pinhole right above the charging port and she only needed to pop the tip of a paper clip in there for five seconds and a secondary menu appeared on the screen that read, Advanced Features - Developer Mode. When in this mode, the device had touch screen capability and when she touched the words, *Developer Mode*, the device notified her:

You are now entering Developer Mode; any changes made in Developer mode not made by a licensed agent may have adverse effects on your device. Are you sure you want to continue?

Scara tapped, **yes**. One of the tracker geeks (probably stalker was more like it), printed a step by step tutorial on reverse look ups for any application that may be tracking the device. Scara smiled as she entered a code when she clicked on **Tracker B.** Her hands had a small tremor as she pecked out the words, all in caps and without any spaces, **REVERSELOOKUP** and then clicked continue. There was a spinning wheel icon on the screen while the device was making up its mind whether or not it was going to follow Scara's command. It was going on ten seconds when the screen flashed blue, a light shade of green and then there was a GPS grid with a glowing blue icon in the far left corner. The blue icon told Scara the exact location of Johnny's phone. And, she didn't know this, but the app on his phone didn't even have to be running for his phone to show active. The app simply needed to be loaded and linked to this device and it met both of those criteria. Scara breathed a sigh of relief, **A.** Because she didn't ruin the device by jail-breaking it and, **B.** Because Johnny wasn't close to her at that time. She had an early warning system as long as he continued to think that it was he tracking her and she wouldn't give him a reason to believe otherwise.

CHAPTER 7

September 15, 2018 – Augusta, GA

Another week had passed since Johnny had seen Scara at Wal-Mart. She followed her normal travel patterns and he figured that he would make his move in a few more days. It was all going down this coming Friday and he had already asked for and gotten the weekend off from Wal-Mart so the time off would be all about winning Scara back. He had everything he needed to get the job done. He tested the GHB that he procured from one of his old sources on himself and that shit knocked him flat on his ass. Gloves, check, leg restraints, check, nylon rope, check. One of the old abandoned Olin chemical cabins at Clarks Hill Lake was almost ready for a party of two. He had to drop by a few more times before it was ready for his lady love. He needed to gas up the generator and make sure that everything powered up when they got there. He had no interest in winning back his love in a woodsy smelling cabin with no electricity. The cabin was equipped with fresh water wells and the showers and toilets were still functional, albeit with cold water.

The GPS tracker alerted Scara every-time Johnny was on the move, and over the last couple of weeks his movements became curiouser and curiouser. She hadn't heard another peep from him except for the night he dropped by to, she imagined, take a look at the device to make sure it didn't need to come off for a charge so she was quick to make sure it was right where he left it. He was going to Clarks Hill Lake with some regularity and Scara did some research on the area. It was, up until three years ago, the camping location for Olin Chemical. Many a birthday party was had there as well as a few wedding receptions. So, why was Johnny going there repeatedly? Scara decided a few days ago that she would have to take a calculated risk. So, she made the decision to leave her Sorento at home with the GPS attached, which meant that she couldn't track Johnny, and Uber over to the campground to take a look around. Hopefully, she didn't pick a time where Johnny would decide he wanted to mosey on over, knowing that Scara was at home, snug as a bug in a rug.

She went late afternoon burgeoning on early evening making an informed guess through her own tracking. The Uber driver that picked her up let her know up front that it was going to be an extended fare because she would have to drive Scara all the way to Appling. Scara assured her driver, Melissa, that she knew it was quite a trek and she had a nice, under the table, cash tip for her and that made Melissa much less hesitant and much more agreeable to enjoy the ride.

Melissa was what Scara would have called a natural beauty. Melissa was blonde with dark brown eyes and she wore no makeup. She had such a pretty face. Her hair was just past shoulder length and it had never been touched by a professional stylist; she was Mama's kitchen all the way. It was parted squarely down the middle and combed neatly even though it was rather plain. Scara wondered what she could do with her in a chair with some mascara and a little blush, maybe some crimson red lipstick. Melissa kept up the small talk and grinned at Scara in the rear-view mirror. This made Scara do a turn in her thinking and thought this was Melissa's charm. She was beautiful in her original packaging. And when Scara really put even a little thought into it; it hit her. Melissa was almost the spitting image of a young Michelle Pfeiffer. After listening to Melissa talk for the better part of forty five minutes, Scara was convinced that this was no act. This was a naive country girl that liked to talk and really had no idea how pretty she actually was. Scara wouldn't be one hundred percent correct in her assessment.

Darkness was about to settle in when they reached the Appling exit and Melissa was talking about the country music concert that her and her Mama saw the weekend before. This was after a twenty minute diatribe on how she got this job with Uber and was grateful to have it because she needed to help her Mama who was on a fixed income since Daddy took ill. Melissa was living all of the elements of a great country song and that southern drawl was so engaging to Scara that she really could have listened to Melissa read the phone book as long as she kept drawing out the syllables.

After getting off at the Appling exit, they took a right turn, passed two bait and tackle shops (both shops were equipped with a griddle and cook to whip up a burger or two for hungry fishermen that came back empty) within a mile of one another before they took a left turn off of the paved road and onto a rough looking dirt one. There was a faded Olin Chemical sign that still stood at the front of the dirt road. Melissa stopped chatting when they turned down the road. She remembered watching a few of those Jason movies as a kid and this was starting to strongly resemble the backdrop of most of them. Melissa slowed her Mitsubishi Montero down to a crawl because Uber wasn't going to pay her shit to have her SUV realigned. The tires moved over the bumpy, gravelly surface of the once well traveled dirt road. Melissa didn't normally ask clients about their business at the destination but it seemed appropriate here because Melissa was beginning to teeter on the edge of being scared shitless. The road got darker the further down they went. She turned on the high beams and could make out a wooden fence that blocked the road and, just beyond the fence, Melissa could make out the cabins that were scattered about the campground. She could see the bath house and a few charcoal pit grills with picnic tables near each one of them and that's when she broke her own rule about asking client business.

"What, what are we doing up here?" Melissa asked.

"I just need to check on something," Scara replied. "I'm going to get out and push the fence open real quick, ok?"

"Hurry up, then. I don't want to be in the paper tomorrow or next month or whenever they find our bodies," Melissa said. She was trying to sound playful but it didn't come out that way. It came out like she was one hundred percent serious. Well, because she was and Scara knew it.

"I don't either; just drive the car in when I push open the fence. Just stay in the car and leave it running. Lock the doors and I'll be right back. Don't you leave me now. If I'm not back in ten minutes or less, drive down to the bait shop and call the police but don't leave me. I'm serious now," Scara said. She didn't move until Melissa responded.

"I won't leave you, you're supposed to give me a fat tip," Melissa replied.

"That's right," Scara said and opened the car door. "Lock the doors, I'll be right back." Scara heard the locks engage as she turned toward the cabins. She pulled the small black Mag-Lite out of her jean pocket and turned the front cap. It lit up the darkness that had been spreading in front of her. "Now Johnny, what have you been doing up here?" Scara shined the light into the first cabin. There seemed to be nothing odd about it; it looked like it hadn't been used since the chemical folks abandoned the site. She moved to the next one and it looked pretty much the same; same with the third cabin. But the fourth cabin...

"This motherfucker," Scara whispered. There was a not so old generator resting on a hard plastic base on the ground outside the fourth cabin. Scara shone the light inside one of the windows and this cabin showed definite signs of recent life. There was a small television sitting on an equally small TV stand in the main room along with a black futon and a worse for wear end table with a Corona bottle lying on its side on top of it. Scara took a closer look at the generator and opened the gas cap. She shone the light into the tank and it had a little bit of gas in the bottom but she was certain that it wasn't enough to power this thing for as long as Johnny would need it. So, he needs to refuel this thing and a thought ran through her head. Maybe she needed to be here waiting on him on his next field trip. He'd never suspect it. Scara knew that this is where he was planning on bringing her. The wheels were turning. He'd want to render her unconscious so he could get her up here to do who knows what (she had a pretty idea of the what but shuddered at the thought) and then he would dump her in the lake when he was done. But, Scara thought, what if I dump his ass in the lake? Nobody would miss this dipshit. The case would grow cold, if a real case was ever opened at all, and she would be the only one to eventually forget all about this bastard.

It was approaching the ten minute mark when she heard Melissa blaring the horn. Scara sprinted back to keep the nervous girl from leaving her alone in the woods. Scara was taking control of the situation but she wasn't stupid. There were plenty of things in these woods that could kill her besides a brainless dipshit seeking revenge.

CHAPTER 8

September 15, 2018 – Clarks Hill Lake

Melissa let it all go on the ride back to Scara's house. This trip became quite personal when Scara had her drive out into the middle of God knows where so she could search for God knows what.

"So, are you going to tell me what that was all about?" Melissa asked. She waited to ask the question until she made the turn onto I-20 East back toward Augusta. Scara spilled a lot of the beans during the long drive back like the beans about having a psycho stalker that she basically sent to prison. And the beans about said stalker getting out and planting a tracking device on her car. She also included the beans about reversing the tracking device and discovering that he had been making frequent trips out to this particular abandoned camp ground. The beans she kept securely in the can were the beans about blowing off Ronald Simpkins face and the love of her life paying for her act in *Gen Pop* of the state penitentiary.

This made Melissa look at Scara through a different lens. She felt sympathy during the story and the pull of anger did grab her for just a moment when she realized that Scara had knowingly put them both in danger. Even though Scara never let Melissa leave the confines of the car, plenty of shit could be done outside of the car to render the car inoperable. Melissa didn't interrupt Scara. She waited until the car was silent again.

"So, are you going to call the police? I mean, you need to call them and they'll throw him right back in."

"I, I don't know what I'm going to do," Scara lied, immediately regretting the beans that she did pour out of the can.

"Well, that's what I would do," Melissa repeated.

"What if I made sure he couldn't hurt me?" Scara asked.

Melissa's ears perked up and before she could help it, a smile broke out under her nose. Scara didn't realize what kind of Uber driver she actually got.

"What would you have in mind?" Melissa parked the car on the curb in front of Scara's house.

"Do you want to come in for coffee or tea?" Scara asked.

"If the tea is sweet, I'll come in. I want to know what you have in mind," Melissa replied.

Scara liked the way the plain looking pretty girl smiled at her. Some connection was made out of thin air and Scara felt a comfort roll over her. Maybe it was Melissa's super enunciated southern drawl. There was just something about this girl that screamed *BEST FRIEND* material. Scara should have just gotten out of the car. She should have just let all of the beans stay in the can.

"The tea is sweet and I would be delighted if you came in for a spell. It's been a long time since I had a long heart to heart with another woman."

"Heart to heart, huh? Is that what we're going to do?" Melissa smiled as she asked. It was only then when Scara realized that this girl had been playing her just a wee bit. She knew exactly how pretty she was and how that natural beauty drove the boys crazy. She saw Melissa drop her cloak of *Awe Shucks and Golly Gee* and begin to reveal a more sly side. The two women walked into the house.

Melissa Rushing took a long, satisfying first drink of the sweet tea that Scara handed over. It flowed blissfully over her tongue and it was close to her mama's tea.

"Ooh, that's good stuff," Melissa said as she pulled the glass from her lips.

"I'm glad you like it," Scara replied. She grabbed a can of Diet Pepsi out of the fridge and the ladies sat on bar stools opposite one another.

"So, let's get back to Mr. Stalker. You say you know where he's going? And you don't want him to hurt you, is that right?"

"Yeah, that's about the size of it," Scara tried to match Melissa's southern charm. It wasn't quite working but it was a solid effort.

"Well, I had a man that used to beat on me and he don't beat on me no more," Melissa said before taking another swig of sweetness.

"Oh shit, that is awful. Was he a stalker?"

"No, nothing like that, I lived with the bastard for six months. Thought we might get married one day. He was as sweet as this tea when we first met up. He was a manager at his job and everything. After going out for about a month, he told me to move in with him. Told me he wanted to take care of me. Help me with my Mama. He was such a gentlemen. All that changed when he got me all moved into his house. I turned into property. He treated me like I was his TV or microwave. Something he used when he was hungry or wanted to be entertained. I remember the first time he hit me like it happened five minutes ago. I came home from work; I had to work later than normal at the Dollar Tree because Willie Simons called in like he frequently did but this time he called in at the end of my shift. So, the manager asked me to stay until she could get one of the overtime hounds, that's what she called them, to come in and cover Willie's shift. So, I did but I didn't call him to let him know and..."

"What was his name?" Scara couldn't stop herself from interrupting.

"Doesn't matter," Melissa replied which implied that it was better if Scara didn't know. Scara didn't press and Melissa continued.

"Well, I called to let him know and he was short with me on the phone. Griping about dinner and that was the first time I'd heard anything resembling a sour word from him. He hung up on me and I didn't think anything else about it. I chalked it up to him having a bad day because we all get one every now and again. So, I'm working at the store about another hour or so when one of the overtime hounds come in, I don't remember which one but one of them came in as quick as they could. I get over to his house, side note, he lives on a country road so he didn't really have neighbors, and he's sitting there in the living room with his work belt draped across the arm of his chair. Again, looking back on it, I wasn't the sharpest tool in the shed because the last thing on my mind was getting hit with that thing. He let me walk into the house. I said something like, 'Hey honey', and he grunted something back to me. Again, I'm thinking bad day, let him have his space. So, I go to the bedroom and start to change out of my work clothes. I'm down to bra and panties and I hear the bedroom door lock. And I'm thinking he just wants sex. Again, not the sharpest tool, I'm thinking I'll let him grunt on top of me for ten minutes if it gets him out of this shit mood and I turn around. He's standing in front of the door with the most evil look that I've ever seen on the face of another human being. He has the belt gripped in his right hand and finally, FINALLY, his intent clicks in my head. That's when fear kicked in. I picked up the closest thing to my hand, which was one of those stiff hairbrushes, you know the old fashioned kind with the solid wood handles, and I threw it as hard and straight as I could. It whacked him right in the middle of his noggin'. He stumbled for just a second and I tried to push past him and get the door unlocked but he was too big and strong for me. He lifted me off the ground like I was a two year old and slammed me face down onto the bed and he went to wailing on me with that belt of his. The first whack hit me in my right shoulder blade and my mind felt like it was dipped in fire. I was screaming for him to stop. I felt my panties being ripped from my bottom, not by his hands but it was the belt ripping them to pieces. I curled up like a baby in her mama's belly and he stopped. I whimpered there for a while and he seemed to get some sick satisfaction from it. He all but told me that I was his property. It was going to be his way or I'd end up missing."

"Oh shit," Scara replied. She realized her situation was bad but it could have been and still could be so much worse. "What did you do?"

Melissa cocked her head, took another drink of tea, dropped her own facade of sweetness and replied, "I killed the motherfucker."

"How, how'd you do it?" Scara couldn't stop the question.

"I set the house on fire with him in it," Melissa answered so nonchalantly that the question could have been, *What did you have for lunch today?*

"The police, what did they say?"

"They couldn't say too much. I had an alibi, well a few actually. My Mama said I was at her house playing Spades with her and Betty Jean. Betty Jean said the same thing. My cell phone said the same thing as they checked the last ping and it was from the tower less than four miles from Mama's house. They asked me to take a lie detector but I declined and since I had my alibis and my phone said I was where I said I was then they had no grounds to arrest me. They suspected arson and I'm sure my name was flung around but, to them, what did I really have to gain? I wasn't the recipient of any insurance money, had no claim to any of his property, no ties with him at all. So, there was nothing for me to gain as far as they were concerned. But, as far as I was concerned, he wouldn't strike me with another belt, or any other woman for that matter. He wouldn't put me in the ground. I was the wrong girl for him to strike. That was for damn sure and even though I did it pretty soon after the beating, I thought it through pretty good. I thought about just going to the police and showing them the beating my ass took. They'd haul him off to jail but what would happen when he made bail because a restraining order ain't nothing but a piece of paper."

Scara thought, *ain't that the truth.*

"So, I'd go ahead and get to the end; an end that was coming for me if I didn't do what I did. I'm certain of that. So, that brings us back to you. What do you want to do about your stalker?"

Scara cocked her head, took a sip of coffee, smiled at Melissa and replied, "I want to kill the motherfucker."

"Alright then," Melissa grinned and they both felt the connection of sisterhood. A friendship that bonded like concrete in the few hours they had known each other.

"I think we get him at the campsite. It's barren for the most part. I think we get him there, paddle him out to the middle of the cove and sink him. Nobody's going to be looking for him," Scara said.

"So, you say you can track him with the device he stuck under your car, that right?"

"Yeah, the trick is I have to take it out to see it."

"Well, let's get it and see how it works. He's using an app, right?" Melissa asked before lifting the glass to her lips once again.

"He does use an app."

"Well, maybe we can download the same app with a different user name. You accessed it through some developer mode, right?"

"That's right," Scara answered and felt immediately stupid for not expanding her investigation. Certainly, the app itself would have the same developer mode. But, could the same device be tracked by the same app on two different phones and that's exactly what Melissa was going to educate her on.

CHAPTER 9

September 17, 2018 – Augusta, GA

Scara downloaded the app and with her new best friend Melissa's help was able to use the developer backdoor to link it to the GPS locator and view the reverse look up. She could activate the developer only feature remotely so she no longer had to remove the locator from the undercarriage of the car to snoop on Johnny. His visits to the campsite were almost daily so far this week so Scara wisely predicted that he was planning to make his move this weekend. It was Wednesday morning and if it went according to plan, dipshit would make his now daily venture out to the site somewhere between 6:00 and 7:00 PM.

"You bout ready to go?" Melissa asked. Scara nodded and smiled at the sound of her friend's deep accent.

"Yeah, let's get it," Scara answered. She hopped into the Montero. It was just past 4:00 PM.

"So, you don't reckon he's going to throw us a curve ball and just show up at your house tonight? That would blow it all to hell, wouldn't it?"

"He's too stupid to throw us a curve ball. He thinks he's got it all figured out. He'll be there," Scara calmly replied.

The pair sat quietly for a little while as Melissa kept the Montero cruising at a steady sixty five miles per hour down I20. Scara replayed the night; the great sex with her husband; the feeling of bliss that her life was when she marched downstairs and into the kitchen for a late night snack; the sound of scratching on the window; the shadow she saw disappear into the shed. She knew it was Johnny. She should have just called the police right then. Why did she have to scream for Jeff? The doors and windows were locked. All she had to do was calmly get her phone and dial 911. Maybe they would have caught him and maybe they wouldn't, but he would have heard the rain of sirens heading his way. And, maybe, just maybe, he would have thought better of all of this shit. He did spend hard time for the last time he fucked with her. Maybe the wail of bubble gum machines would have made him rethink his life. But no, Scara had to scream. Jeff had to barrel downstairs with gun in hand like she knew no doubt that he would. The silence was crushing her but she deserved it. She wasn't going to break it; she was going to face it. It would have been easy to break the silence like a stone through wet paper. Her lips wanted to break it; wanted to start up another conversation with Melissa but her brain wouldn't allow it. It forced Scara to continue down memory lane. The shotgun in the closet. How she expertly loaded the shells and cocked the first one. Scara, why couldn't you just calm the fuck down? Daddy told you a thousand times, *See What You Shoot!* Scara remembered the splintering of wood followed by that awful gargling noise. She heard Ronald before she saw him. That gargling sound would never leave her. She could see his face; his teeth were shattered and scattered shards down his pajama shirt and what was left of his jaw was hanging like a broken door hinge. His eyes were wide and blinking with disbelief. The blood was oozing from the opening where his mouth used to be like the steady flow of an active volcano. The silence was going to break her but Scara wouldn't break it. Jeff took the gun away from her and looked into her eyes; told her that he loved her and that she needed to listen to him. She did and she wished with everything she had that she hadn't. They didn't even give poor Ronald a chance to live. Sure, it looked bad; it looked bleak as fuck but modern medicine can do many miraculous things now. Rebuild a jaw? The single shell hadn't collapsed Ronald's skull. That would be the one Jeff put into him. So, by the book, Jeff did put the shot in him that took Ronald's last gurgling breath but it was Scara that put him in that spot. She killed Ronald, Jeff just cleaned up her mess. Finally, mercifully, the silence was broken.

"Hey, why are you crying? We don't have to do this. I can drive you to the police station and we can just report him," Melissa said. She was ready to flip the blinker and get off at the next exit to turn around.

"No, I don't want to go to the police. I want to kill him and make it like he never existed."

"That's the spirit," Melissa removed her hand from the blinker until fifteen minutes later when they approached Exit 183 for Appling, GA.

The women entered the campsite and unloaded at the cabin next to the one that Johnny was occupying. Melissa moved the Montero. She parked it six cabins down and a little ways into the wooded area behind the last cabin. Johnny wouldn't have a need to drive back that far. He had everything he needed setup in his cabin.

Scara scuttled through the window near the generator and Melissa checked the gas to find it full and thought about firing it up but decided against it. Johnny might feel the heat from it when he gets here and get suspicious. Melissa left it as cold as she found it.

"Oh my God," Scara said. Johnny had been up to quite a bit since they had been here last. Scara was standing in the bedroom and there was a full size bed sitting on a platform bed frame butted up against the far wall. Attached to each bed post were thick leather restraints meant for wrists and ankles.

"Oh my God is right, we do need to deep six this motherfucker," Melissa said angrily.

Scara's phone gave a ding. Johnny was on the move. She opened the app with Melissa looking over her shoulder.

"He's still forty minutes out but he's on the way," Scara said.

"Well, let's make sure we have our shit together."

"Ok."

Johnny was singing along with George Thorogood letting everyone know that he was "*Buhbuhbuhbuh Bad to the Bon*e" as he turned onto the Interstate. Just this week, he had taken up semi-permanent residency at the abandoned Olin campsite. Got a great deal on a generator from his employer; the employee discount was definitely a perk and the free in store pick up. Well, Wally World just has to be the finest retail establishment in the world. Johnny glanced at his phone but the app hadn't come to life. Scara must be staying in tonight. Good for her, Johnny thought. She would need her rest. He had big plans for them this weekend. They would reconcile and when they left the campsite together, all would be right with the world. She'd look at him the way she looked at that tall drink of water that she was with. He wasn't right for her. And Johnny thought about that night himself. He turned off the radio so he could sit in the silence and remember how fortunate he was to get Jeff out of the picture without really doing much of anything. A little trespassing, a passing glimpse that Scara caught him in and the rest of it just worked itself out. Karma was finally smiling on him for a change. The nosy neighbor getting blown away was the coup de gras. That blast was meant for him and that made him smile even wider.

"That bitch was really going to kill me," Johnny whispered.

Johnny pulled into the campsite. He took a deep breath of the lake air and headed toward the generator. He started it up and the lights in the living area of the cabin sprang to life. He lifted the window and expertly crawled in like he'd been slipping in and out of windows all of his life. He took a quick peek into the bedroom and he could almost see Scara lying there waiting on him. He kicked off his shoes and moved to the living area. He felt a warm sting in his neck and swatted at it. At first, he thought it was an errant yellow jacket. He realized as consciousness faded away that it was no insect at all. He could see a hazy silhouette of a shapely woman...no, not one but two of them...what the hell? Johnny went nighty-night.

Johnny was woozy and his head was throbbing. He started to raise his hand to his temple and his wrist snapped back with a sudden stop. His mind woke up pretty quickly after that. He lifted both of his hands and they were held tightly by the restraints, the restraints he installed. He kicked his feet and they were secured just as tightly as his wrists. Johnny saw the women standing side by side in the doorway of the bedroom.

"You've been a busy little bee, haven't you, Johnny?" Scara asked. She moved slowly to the foot of the bed.

"Who's the looker?" Johnny asked. He was taking in Melissa's natural beauty.

"A friend of mine."

"I haven't seen her before," Johnny said as he relaxed his pull on the restraints.

"Oh, we just met a few days ago," Melissa said.

"Well, I'll be, are we going to have a threesome?" Johnny asked. He didn't understand how grave his predicament was. He was already playing it all out in his head. The, *If you ever come near me again, it will end much worse for you, blah, blah, blah,* they weren't gonna' do shit.

"Oh yeah, baby. We're going to have a threesome. You'll be screaming for mercy when we really get going," Melissa said. She moved closer to the head of the bed and Scara remained at the foot.

"I like her, Scara. She's what I call a natural beauty. Not a lot of cover up on her face. Pretty little thing," Johnny was talking as if he were looking at a pinup in a magazine.

"She is a natural beauty, Johnny. But, she can also be a beast," Scara snarled when she said it and this change in her face made Johnny flinch. It made him know that this wasn't going to be a, *teach him a lesson* moment. With that snarl, he knew he was in very real trouble. And he quickly remembered the shotgun blast, *the bitch was gonna' kill me.*

Melissa pulled the hunting knife from its sheath and held it close to her face. It covered the bridge of her nose and the front of her mouth. All Johnny could see of Melissa's face were her eyes and a few teeth on each side of the blade.

"Hey, you girls have had your fun," he started.

"Oh no, no, no, Johnny. We haven't had our fun. We haven't had our threesome yet. The fun has hardly begun. Don't tell me you're a quick draw. You're not a quick draw, are you, Johnny?" Melissa asked; her face still obscured by the serrated blade of the hunting knife.

"Look, Scara. I'm sorry about your husband and all but you know that shit wasn't my fault. Nobody told him to shoot that man. I wasn't even near your front porch. I mean, it was an accident, what the fuck, Scara?" Johnny's brave front; the bully that pushed Kevin around at Wally World was all gone now. His true self was making a rare appearance. He turned into a sniveling jackal that was trying to say anything to get out of his current situation.

76

"I suppose those leather straps on your wrists and feet were accidents too, huh, dipshit? I suppose you just needed those so you could sleep flat on your back, that it? I'm sure you weren't going to moan on top of me while I kicked and wiggled under your foul body. You weren't going to do any of that, were you?" Scara was getting angrier with every sentence and Johnny's eyes widened.

"Look, I wasn't going to do that. I just wanted to scare you a little bit. I wasn't going to force myself on you like that. I was just salty about going to jail. That's all. I just wanted to get even."

"Even? Even steven? Well, if you want to get even steven then I need to call the police now and have you taken back to jail for stalking me."

"Call them. It's my fault," Johnny's lips began trembling. Melissa moved the knife closer to his face and she whispered to him, "I think she wants more than even steven. After what you put her through, I think more than even steven is appropriate. We still need to have our threesome...and Johnny; you can't be a quick draw."

He felt the sting again, once again followed by darkness.

"Help me get the straps off of him," Melissa said. Scara moved quickly and loosened his wrists while Melissa worked on his feet.

"Ok, let's get him out of here."

Scara grabbed Johnny by his arms and Melissa grabbed his legs. The women pulled him from the bed and walked him back out of the open front door and, once they were walking on the dirt ground,

Scara dropped his arms and grabbed one of Johnny's feet. Melissa and Scara dragged Johnny across the rugged ground to the waiting jon boat. The woods around them picked up a little noise from the wind; it started its rustle in the east and was now moving across their faces.

"You sure you want to go through with it?" Melissa asked. It was not out of concern for herself; her own face showed that she was A-ok with the current course of action.

"I do," Scara replied. They heaved Johnny into the boat and Scara pulled the chain to her chest.

"Wrap them around his feet like I showed you and push the padlock through," Melissa said.

Scara dutifully obeyed while Melissa pulled the pillowcase over Johnny's head.

"Alright then, hand over one of them paddles," Melissa directed. Scara exhaled and her heart picked up the pace. Dusk was approaching and they needed to get this done so the world could begin forgetting the memory of Johnny Pickens. The women paddled in unison until they were just outside the comfort of the campsite's cove.

"That point," Melissa said as she raised her hand.

"Got it," Scara replied. A trolling motor would have been a big help right then but they would have to do it the old fashioned way. Johnny was curled in a chained up ball on the floor of the boat.

"Think he'd help us paddle?" Scara jokingly asked.

"You wanna' wake him up and find out," Melissa replied with no humor in her voice. She was in serious mode at that moment. Melissa wasn't there to fuck around.

The women paddled until Scara's arms were just beginning to feel the burn. The sun was descending although it was still above the water line. The women were in the open water of Clarks Hill Lake. Melissa stopped paddling and Scara followed suit.

"I think this is good enough," Melissa said.

Scara spun around in the jon boat, checking out the shoreline as carefully as she could to make sure that an errant fisherman or some curious kid weren't watching them from a bank or another boat elsewhere. There was a hawk circling overhead, certainly about to bring death from the sky to some unsuspecting squirrel or reptile. Scara took a deep breath and looked into Melissa's eyes.

"Ok, let's dump this sack of shit," Scara said.

Melissa grinned.

"Ok, grab the block and slide it toward me, I'll heave him up and over but that block has got to go right behind him, understand?"

"I do," Scara replied. It was as if she were dancing in a daydream. The surreal calm swept over Scara as she moved to do what she was told. There was no turning back. She was committed and she wanted to be committed.

Scara slid the cement block. Melissa straddled Johnny as he lay motionless. She reached around his midsection and lifted with her knees. He was lying on his back and she could feel the steady rhythm of his breath coming through the pillow case. He wasn't all that heavy and she got him almost in a seated position to the edge of the boat. Their weight caused the small boat to list to the heavier side.

"Ok, I'm going to dump his ass over and I need that block to go out right behind him before we run out of chain," Melissa said and tugged hard around Johnny's waist. She had his butt clearing the side.

"You fucking bitch," is what she heard through the pillowcase. Melissa gave a hard push while Scara simultaneously slid the block from the edge and sent it tumbling into the dark water, taking chain with it. She grinned as she turned back to Melissa; a grin that turned to horror.

Johnny was roused awake and he felt the woman's arms around his waist. He was still groggy but he knew was in some pretty deep shit. His hands were cuffed and his feet were bound but he had movement in is bony legs. He felt the body of a woman that was obviously not Scara press into him. The women made what turned out to be a fatal flaw when they moved him from the bed. They restrained his wrists in the front instead of behind his back but they really didn't anticipate him waking up and that underestimation was about to cost them. Johnny opened his legs as she pressed into him. She was sliding him and he could hear the lap of water all around him and then he heard Scara's voice. The woman had him to the edge of the boat and as she gave one last push, he scissored his legs around her and clamped them and said, "You fucking bitch." Then he shot his cuffed hands straight out and gripped the belt-line of Melissa's jeans.

There was a rush of coldness that brought him out of whatever fog was left by the shit they gave him. The woman was flailing about. He kept the grip on her waist with his tightly clamped knees and an even tighter grip with his hands on the inside of her jeans. Johnny knew this was going to be his final resting place so he was going to take this bitch with him. She was struggling but Johnny refused to loosen his grip. Then there was a sudden pull at his feet; like an ancient shark living in the deep waters of the lake had suddenly erupted from the depths to bring down its dinner. The woman wriggled. In the underwater struggle, she pulled the pillowcase away from Johnny's face. He leaned in and did the most primal thing that he could do. He bit down hard into the flesh of her arm and kept his grip down below. Blood flowed from the wound as the pair descended into the silence.

Scara's instinct overtook her and she dove into the water. She didn't register the stinging cold. Scara looked like a svelte mermaid in the dark water of the lake, an outline of beauty in the calm blackness. She stayed under the water moving and reaching. Her eyes could see nothing and there was an engulfing silence. A silence that attached itself; a silence that, in those moments of desperation became a part of her; a part of her that would whisper in the darkness; a part of her that would make her see things; a part of her that would want to destroy itself just to claim her. The silence began growing inside of her on this very day.

Melissa fought. She kicked as they were rapidly sinking to the bottom of the lake. She was disoriented and had lost all sense of direction; up was down and down was up. Johnny still had a grip on her. The panic subsided and what was merely seconds felt like long minutes; minutes without oxygen cycling to her brain. Melissa reached for the waistband of her jeans. Johnny still had a firm grip on them. Melissa stilled herself and unbuttoned the jeans and slid the zipper. They slipped off like the peel from a banana. Johnny finally took a gasping breath of lung filling water.

Melissa kicked, that was her instinct. The vertigo of silence overwhelmed her. Then, she swam; she kicked and moved her arms like pistons. Melissa was fighting off the involuntary need to take a breath. The brief fight with Johnny had literally almost depleted all of the air in her lungs. Melissa felt as if they may burst into flames unless she sucked in the water; flood the lungs and put out the flames of her life. She didn't want to die. She wasn't going to die. She was going to make it to the surface. She and Scara could huddle up in the cabin and have a laugh. She could warm up and get a blanket to put around her bare ass. Scara could run into one of those bait shops, grab them a quick bite and a couple of drinks. All of this ran through Melissa's mind as she scrambled for the surface. Her body made her take an unwanted breath and Melissa felt the water rush down her windpipe just as she broke the surface. She could see the boat. She could see Scara climbing back into it. Melissa was trying to wave and splash but the lake had sapped her. She had to expel the water from her lungs. Scara couldn't see or hear her. Melissa didn't know that the silence had now claimed Scara. The silence wouldn't let her ears hear her as she splashed about. Melissa threw up the water in her lungs and she began a labored swim to shore. Scara grabbed a paddle and was rowing away. Melissa couldn't find her voice. She tried to yell out but a gurgled mix of air and water is what came out. It was going to be ok. Scara would wait on her once she got to shore. She'd wait for Melissa to show up and everything would work out. Melissa continued her swim to the nearest shoreline– a shoreline that was nothing but sharp rocks with dense woods just beyond its reach.

Scara was numb. Melissa was gone. Scara picked up a paddle and began cutting the boat back through the water. She had succumbed to the silence and was in its complete grip as she paddled back the way they had come. The sun was just about to fall below the waterline and signal the end of the day. Scara was so consumed that she didn't even remember grabbing the car keys that Melissa left on the bedside table and driving away in Melissa's Montero or parking it in an empty church parking lot five blocks from her own house. When Scara woke up the next morning, she had almost convinced herself that it was all a bad dream.

CHAPTER 10

September 17, 2018 – Clarks Hill Lake

Melissa was freezing. She trudged through the woods. Good thing she was a country girl and the woods didn't really scare her all that much. She knew what to look for and her sense of direction was keen; probably one of the traits that made her such a great Uber driver. She moved quickly as the sun had just set but there was still just a bit of ambient light left in the sky. Her arms were catching the dickens (her right arm especially with Johnny's fresh teeth marks); her limbs poking out here and there. She was getting scratched up but it was ok, she would surprise Scara at the cabin. She just hoped that Scara hadn't done something rash like call the police. Neither one of them needed that. She could see herself emerging from the woods, pants-less with Scara standing there wide eyed talking to a cop with an open notebook telling him everything that she and her newly deceased friend had just done except, the friend wasn't deceased. The friend was very much alive and didn't want to go to jail for murdering a piece of shit like Johnny. Melissa went on sort of an auto pilot of her own. The country girl moved expeditiously through the woods. She smiled when she could see the light from the cabin. Melissa broke into a run. She didn't see the Montero but she did see Johnny's motorcycle. She'd have to push that into the woods after she warmed up a bit.

Maybe Scara went for help. Melissa's cell phone was lost with her pants. She walked into the empty cabin. Melissa would just wait. Surely, Scara would come back in a little while. Probably with the police so Melissa needed to be thinking of a credible story that she could feed a cop to keep suspicion away from her and her new friend. She pulled off her shirt. She was freezing so she crawled into the bed that Johnny was tied up in and curled up under the blankets. She would listen out for the car; Scara would be there any minute. Melissa continued to think that until she dozed off. She woke up three hours later.

"That bitch left me."

———

Scara just stared out of the window. She was living a nightmare. Johnny was dead but he took Melissa with him and Scara couldn't say a word. She'd just watch the news and wait for them to talk about the missing young woman. She'd harbor this secret right beside the other one. So now the death toll was two innocents for one dipshit. Scara removed the tracking device from underneath her car and smashed it to pieces with a hammer. She removed the app from her phone. Scara went to work and pretended like there was nothing out of the ordinary. The Montero was in the church parking lot the first day she drove by. It wasn't there on day two. On day two, the parking spot that she left it in was empty. Scara made sure she stayed alert on social media and definitely tuned into the local news. There wasn't a single mention of a young lady missing from the area. Maybe the church had the car towed.

Maybe the pastor saw it in the parking lot for an extended period and maybe that bothered him enough to call the towing company. That was a few too many maybes for Scara. She broke down and decided to call Melissa's number to see if there was an answer. There was.

"Well, hello stranger," Melissa answered.

"Oh my, thank God you're alive."

"No thanks to you, bitch. How could you leave me like that? I mean, seriously. I almost died and you were just going to leave me out there like that."

"I, I was afraid. I didn't know what to do so I panicked, ok. I'm sorry, I'm just glad you're ok."

"Look that was messed up. I walked back through the woods in a sopping wet shirt with no pants to get back to the cabin. I just knew you'd be there waiting on me. I thought you might panic and call the cops or something but I expected you to be there at least for a little while waiting on me and when I got there, I got nothing but an empty cabin and hope for your return. I fell asleep waiting on you and woke up in the middle of the night. I kind of got the hint that you hadn't called the police or had any intention of coming back for me yourself."

"Look," Scara tried to interject.

"No, no look, I'm not done yet. You didn't come back for me; didn't have any intention of coming back for me. You were just going to let my body drift away and let my family worry about where I was. That's pretty shitty for someone that said that they were my friend. The funny thing about it is, after my shirt somewhat dried out and I found some guys old swim trunks in the back of the closet, I walked to the first bait shop and had to use the shop phone to call a cab. I couldn't even call an Uber because my phone was at the bottom of the lake and cabs cost a shit ton. You owe me eighty bucks for that cab ride, by the way…oh, and another sixty for my new phone."

"I'm so, so sorry, I'm just glad you're ok," Scara replied. She was on the brink of sobbing.

"I'm ok, Scara but you're not a very good friend so I think we can just leave it at that."

"Melissa, I didn't know what to do, I'm so..."

"Just stop with the sorries and don't call me again. Call me again and I'll have to block you. Communicate with me in any other way and maybe the law has to get involved. Just leave me alone," Melissa said and hung up.

Scara stared at her phone in disbelief. Was her instinct for self preservation really that strong? Strong enough where she would let the love of her life spend time in prison for her and strong enough to leave a new friend for dead at the bottom of a lake. Scara had to accept the reality that it positively was. The silence was creeping into her mind and she thought of Scotland. She was going to take the trip. She was going to get away. She was going to clear her mind and come back with a renewed purpose but the silence kept hammering her and she kept pushing back. Edinburgh would give her something that she was lacking. The trip meant for her and Jeff would put her back on track for her life; make her ready for when he came back to her; make her a better person. So, why did she have the certain feeling that the silence would follow her to the ends of the earth to claim her? Scara fumbled through the medicine cabinet and found the Xanax that Dr. Blake prescribed her shortly after Jeff went to his new home. She shook the bottle and heard two of the pills bouncing around inside. She took them both and chased them down with Diet Coke. She'd call Dr. Blake tomorrow and have him call in another prescription. Maybe she'd go see David at The Book Tavern. The new Stephen King book was coming out and she really wanted to visit the shop to buy that one. It was called *The Institute* and maybe that's where she belonged. Some sort of a mental institution because what normal person would do the shit that Scara had done?

"I'll keep the trip," she said out loud. "I'll keep the trip and I'll come home and wait for Jeff," Scara set the phone down and went to call her mother. She needed to hear someone tell her that she was a good person. She wasn't really a good person; she was a shitty person and the silence was coming for her.

Six weeks had passed since the cabin incident and even though that much time had gone by, Melissa tinkered with the idea of just going to the cops anyway. Scara really would have just let her die at the bottom of the lake. Even though they hadn't known each other very long, Melissa thought she was a much better judge of character. She had been through her own shit with men in the past and she knew that a restraining order was as useless as the paper it was printed on. Melissa didn't want to bear any guilt if this man came back and killed this woman. The thing was, he wouldn't just kill her. A lot of things would have happened judging by the way his cabin was set up than just killing Scara. Melissa was more than happy to rid the world of this slime ball. And this bitch was just going to leave her in the lake; just let her mother worry about her. Melissa could have let it go if Scara had made any attempt at saving her, any attempt at letting someone know. This, this she just couldn't let go.

CHAPTER 11

July 22, 2020: 4:12 AM – Augusta, GA

Melissa woke up in a cold sweat. That day affected her more than she would ever admit. She would have dreams of drowning at least four to five times a month. She would wake when she felt the water invade her lungs. Melissa didn't tell another soul about what happened that day on the lake with Scara. Melissa took some time off from driving folks around after that day. Scara tried to call her a couple of times (even after Melissa's stern warning) but never left a message or a text. After a couple of unanswered calls, Melissa figured that Scara had finally got the message.

She was up and ready to go. Today was the day that she could get her passport. Melissa had a somewhat last minute trip planned. She sat down in front of the laptop that never moved from the small desk in her bedroom and opened the PDF that she had downloaded the week before. The document was entitled, *The Burryman Festival, South Queensferry: Warding off Evil Spirits, Connecting With Nature, and Celebrating Local Identity*, and the title page had the Semper Clausus shield and armor pictured.

Melissa had read through the document several times and had even reached out to gain more information on the Burryman festival. Her email was promptly answered with a quick and distinct description of The Burryman's Day:

Melissa,

Thank you for your interest in the Burryman Festival. The Burryman's Day always happens on the 2nd Friday after the 1st Saturday in August in a little village called South Queensferry. He gets dressed in burrs by a team of his helpers at 7:45 AM in the local pub called the Stag Head hotel. This is where he starts and finishes his day. He leaves here at 8:45 AM and returns at 6:00 PM. After he departs in the morning, he walks round the whole of South Queensferry receiving whisky from the community bringing good luck to everyone he meets. This is the route he takes.

The Route

Please note that all times are approximate and subject to change.

Time	Location	Time	Location	Time	Location
08.45	Leave Staghead Hotel	11.40	Rosebery Court	14.40	Bridges Pool Hall
09.00	Villa Road (first drink at the Provost's house)	11.45	Lawson Crescent	14.45	The Toppies
09.20	Farquhar Terrace	11.50	Queen Margaret Drive	15.00	Lovers Lane (west end)
09.30	Walker Drive	12.05	Rosebery Avenue (west end)	15.05	Kirkliston Road
09.35	Bo'ness Road (bottom)	12.15	The Haven	15.10	The Varnies via Hope St
09.40	Springfield View	12.30	William Black Place/ Dundas Avenue (west end)	15.20	Viewforth Place
09.45	Springfield Road			15.25	Kirkliston Road
09.55	Springfield Crescent			15.30	The Loan/ Scotmid
10.00	Echline Gardens	12.35	Stewart Clark Avenue	15.55	Morison Gardens
10.15	Echline Grove	12.45	Almond Grove	16.00	The Inchcolm Inn
10.30	Cross Roads / Stewart Terrace	13.00	Wellhead Close	16.20	The High Street
		13.15	Sommerville Gardens	16.40	Honeypot Ceramics
10.50	Station Road	13.25	Provost Milne Grove (lunch)	16.55	The Hawes Inn
11.10	Whitehead Grove / Ashburnham Rd			17.10	The Three Bridges
		14.15	Scotstoun Avenue	17.30	The Anchor Inn
11.20	Queensferry Rugby Club/ Dundas Avenue (east end)	14.20	Scotstoun Park (east end)	17.40	The Ferry Tap
				17.45	The Boat House
		14.25	Arup (Scotstoun House)	17.50	Maisie's Boutique
11.35	Rosebery Avenue (east end)	14.35	Scotstoun Park (west end)	17.55	Orocco Pier
				18.00	The Staghead Hotel

One other thing that I should mention is that whilst the Burryman is going around South Queensferry, Cameron and Seth, our bell-ringers, ring the bells shouting, "HIP, HIP HOORAY! IT'S THE BURRYMAN'S DAY!" There is a video on Youtube from CNN who came over a few years back and spent some time with us. I have sent you the link in a separate email. The Ferry Fair begins the day after the Burryman's march and continues through the following Saturday. They have different activities every night for people to take part and then on the Saturday it's "Ferry Fair" day where children in all the schools in South Queensferry get chosen to be part of the queens procession. I hope this information has helped you with your paper on our beloved festival. Please don't hesitate to email me with any other questions that you may have around the Burryman Festival, Ferry Fair or anything related to South Queensferry.

Claire

Melissa read all forty plus pages of the attached document and studied the route of the Burryman. Scara had kept her trip. It was time for them to reconnect. It was time to make amends. Melissa felt the tug of the silence. There was one aspect of the Burryman that Melissa found most interesting. It was the one aspect that, according to what she has read, was the unpopular purpose of the Burryman – The Scapegoat. That seemed more than appropriate to Melissa – a place to lay your burden and cleanse yourself. She hadn't known Scara that long but she figured out who she truly was on that day. She was caring until she wasn't. She was thoughtful until it was time for self preservation and then all bets were off. And here is a figure in walking form, a figure outside of Jesus Christ himself that can be approached and soiled. Melissa got the sense that the Scotland trip was supposed to be somewhat therapeutic for Scara – something to gain forgiveness or atonement. She reread the last email from Claire (no last name given) and decided she would respond.

Claire,

Thank you for the information on The Burryman Festival and the Ferry Fair. I have until the end of the school year to finish my thesis on the festival. What I'm asking is, and I know it's a big ask because you don't really know me, well, can I call you or Facetime you? Are you on Facebook? I'm scheduling a trip out there just before the week of Ferry Fair. I'd like to talk to

someone local so I can get the skinny on the best hotel to stay at on a budget in South Queensferry. I want to follow the route of the Burryman on that Friday if possible. I think seeing all of this firsthand would really enhance what I am putting in my thesis and show a true dedication to my professor. He is very tough to impress and earning a good grade in his course isn't a small task. This will go a long way into helping me and will enlighten me on a piece of history that I can always say that I witnessed; a story that I can pass down to my children and my children's children. To tell them the tale of the Burryman straight from my lens may encourage them to take trips to your fine land over the years and experience what I hope to experience. If you are on Facebook, I have included a link to my profile page, just shoot me a friend request and I will accept ASAP. I look forward to hearing from you, Claire. Even more, I look forward to meeting you very soon. Thank you again for all of your help.

Melissa Rushing

Only eight minutes passed when Melissa heard the ding on her phone which signaled a Facebook notification. She had received a friend request from Claire Giblet. Melissa smiled and accepted. She immediately got the prompt to *wave* at her new Facebook friend. Melissa opened messenger and saw the moving "..." that signaled a message was being formulated.

Hi, Melissa, it's Claire Giblet. I would be more than happy to Facetime with you. Is now a good time?

Claire, hi, yes, perfect. Give me five minutes and I'll call you.

I'll be waiting.

Melissa took a quick appearance check in the mirror. Her hair wasn't too crazy and her bedroom was picked up for the most part. She pressed the phone icon in messenger. It rang a few times before she saw a young, sandy blonde haired woman smiling back at her. Melissa had pictured in her mind that a pale redhead would answer but how about that, another stereotype smashed.

"Claire?" Melissa politely questioned.

"Of course, it's Claire. So, tell me when you were coming out? I can pick you up when you arrive if you would like."

Melissa pushed back her smile. She loved the Scottish accent and she liked Claire right off the bat. The last time she had such a great feeling about someone right off the bat; it didn't turn out all that well. She ended up left for dead, soaking wet and practically naked so she'd be a little cautious with her new overseas friend.

"Well, hey there. You are really pretty, I'm sorry just taken aback for a second."

"Oh, now you caught me off guard. Thank you," Claire's smile filled the laptop screen.

I'm finalizing the booking so I don't have an exact day and time that I will arrive as of yet but I will have that by tomorrow. I may take you up on the ride. Where should I stay? Can I stay at the Stag Head?"

"Stag Head is more of a pub. There are a few rooms up top but my recommendation would be The High Street or The Hawes Inn. They are both on the Burryman's route and both are fine hotels. If you pressed me though, I'd take Hawes over High Street but Hawes is a little pricier. Their restaurant is fabulous."

"Ok, I guess I can book either of those online then."

"Yes, you certainly can. Go take a look at the rooms. If you have any specific questions around them let me know. I'm not volunteering this without talking with my husband but let me speak with him and see if he would be up to letting you stay in our guest room. That would save you some money."

"Oh no, I couldn't do that. You don't know me outside of a couple of emails and our talk right now. I wouldn't dream of imposing on you and your husband."

"I understand. How about once you get here and stay in Hawes a couple of nights, we all get to know each other and if it's a fit, then you can finish your stay with us. That will still save you some money. I know that is quite a journey and a penny saved is a penny earned."

"Yeah, that's what we say but most Americans don't live that way. As a country we spend money we don't have and run everything on those plastic cards. Those plastic cards get a lot of us in real trouble. They look innocent enough though, don't they? Just little rectangle cards you stick in machines made for them and you magically get to take the merchandise home or eat the meal or stay in the room or get on the plane...you get my drift?"

"Drift?"

"You understand my meaning?"

"Yes, absolutely. The more reason you can use the room once we get comfortable with each other. I'll speak with Shane and I'll Facetime you tomorrow around this time. Would that be good?" Claire asked.

Melissa could see the open area behind Claire's shoulder. She was standing in a very nice kitchen. "That would be great. I look forward to talking with you tomorrow. In the meantime, I'll get my flight and hotel itinerary finalized. It was great speaking with you and thanks again for all of your help. This paper is going to be out of this world."

"You are so welcome. I'll talk to you tomorrow. Take care, goodbye," Claire said and disconnected the call.

Melissa's next call was with Delta Airlines. She spent the better part of the next hour getting her flight booked. She paid for it with a new American Express card; a card that she really shouldn't have applied for but she wouldn't have been able to afford this trip any other way. She could have taken out one of those online loans but the interest rate would have had her paying it off for years so Melissa chalked it up as American Express loaning her the money and after the trip, the card could be locked away somewhere while she made the monthly payments. After booking the flight, Claire's offer to stay at their place was looking like a really good option. Too bad she didn't intend to be there that long.

CHAPTER 12

July 28, 2020: 8:22 AM – Atlanta, GA

Scara Slayfield turned over in her bed and glared at the empty pillow. Every morning, Scara felt a twinge of guilt in her gut. Jeff was in prison because he protected her. Scara hadn't had a good night's sleep since Jeff was sentenced. They were supposed to take a romantic trip to Edinburgh, Scotland and the time for that trip was fast approaching. Scara still had the plane tickets and a reservation for two at the High Street Hotel that were now non-refundable.

Scara rolled out of bed and her feet hit the cold, hardwood floor. The chill opened her eyes a bit. She moved sloth-like to the bathroom where the mirror stopped her. She moved toward it as tears filled her eyes. She could almost feel Jeff's arms wrap around her. Her dark eyes were becoming pools and she moved her long, black hair from in front of her face. The worry lines on her forehead would one day stick if she didn't find some relief from her grief and depression. Jeff wasn't dead for God's sake but he wasn't here and he wasn't going to be here for a long time.

Scara brushed her teeth quickly to kill the dragon breath that filled her mouth during the restless night. She turned on the shower and waited until she could see the steam rise above the curtain before she pulled off her pajamas and stepped inside. Her cell phone began to ring and she thought to herself that she would return the call. It was Jeff and he had news. She missed the call and there wouldn't be another one.

Three days before leaving for Scotland.

The sleepless nights were more frequent the closer it was time for Scara to fly out of Georgia. She hadn't been able to get through to Jeff since she missed his call the other morning. She wanted to talk to him before she left. She wanted to let him know that she was going to miss him; that she wanted him to be with her so badly. Scara had been researching South Queensferry and had figured out that Jeff was more than likely taking her somewhere on the Burryman festival's route. Scara read up a tiny bit on the festival, but her real learning would come when she actually got there and met Andrew and even more when she met the elderly gentleman, George.

Today, she was checking in with her mother to make sure that Sheena was all set to stay with her. Sheena would be low maintenance, just feed her, keep the litter box clean and that was it. Even though Scara had been in this apartment for almost four months, she was still adjusting to life in downtown Atlanta. She had gotten a job with a local marketing firm. She was made for it with her good looks and her outgoing personality, which bubbled its way back to the top when she could block out the shit that had gone down with Johnny and Melissa. Well, she had definitely gotten over Johnny but Melissa was another story. Melissa was haunting her thoughts. That moment, in the dark water, is where the silence fully committed to her and her to it. Sure, when she pulled the trigger of the shotgun, the silence came to her and when Jeff was sentenced, it knocked on the door. But...when she dove into the dark water, it kicked the door in. And it was beckoning her. Scara tried to convince herself that she needed this getaway. She needed to get out of the country and focus on drowning the silence instead of vice versa. Scara called her sister.

Lisa was waiting in the checkout line at Circle K when her phone started to buzz and when she saw her sister's name she quickly answered.

"Hey, girl!" Lisa shouted. The middle aged woman in front of her in line turned and gave her an appalled look. It took some effort for Lisa not to smile and give her the single finger salute. The fake disdain left the woman's face when the cashier told her that she was next.

"I catch you at a bad time?" Scara asked.

"No, I'm at Circle K where apparently people get pissed when you answer your phone," Lisa said loud enough to elicit another look from the woman. Lisa was sure that Mrs. Prudeface was going home to prepare for some sort of midday tea party with her snootie patootie friends.

"I can call you back," Scara said.

"No, it's good. One second though," Lisa said. Scara heard the cashier tell Lisa that her total was seventeen eighty two and she heard Lisa curse at the debit card as the chip reader didn't work on the first push. She heard some crumpling and then Lisa was back.

"Sorry about that. What's up?"

"I'm just touching base. You know, I leave in a couple of days. I took Sheena over to Mom's and I just want to make sure that you are going to stop by and check on her and the cat."

"Oh, yeah, it's not like I don't see Mom every day. You need to come over tomorrow night for dinner. I'm cooking."

"That sounds good, what are you cooking?"

"Well, I'm making lasagna."

"Oh, well count me in," Scara said. Lisa was the real cook in the family. She could have been a chef if she really set her mind to it but went into real estate instead.

"Lasagna, a side salad, some garlic bread an you can bring the wine," Lisa said.

"I will."

"How are you, sis?" Lisa asked, her tone became less light and more serious.

"I'm doing alright, I guess, it's just been hard without Jeff, you know."

"Are you sure you should be taking this trip alone? It's a long trip without a familiar face."

"I've had second and third thoughts about it, but I think I need to go and I think going alone may be the best thing for me. Just forget everything for a little while and refocus my life, you know. Jeff will be home in a couple of years and I just need this, I think. Hell, I don't know. It may be the worst thing that I could do but I won't know unless I just do it. It's somewhere I've always wanted to go. You remember my obsessions."

"That I do…you and Joey, both." There was an awkward silence before Lisa continued, "Call me if you need anything. I'm showing a house in thirty minutes and I'm twenty minutes away from it. I'll see you tomorrow and don't forget the wine."

"I won't forget the wine, love you."

"Love you too, bye."

Scara suddenly felt the need to cry so she did. It helped.

CHAPTER 13

August 6, 2020: 5:00 PM – Dinner at Rosalie's

Scara arrived at her mother's promptly at 5:00 PM with a bottle of *Winking Owl* wine – it was inexpensive wine but it was very good. Sheena was waiting by the front door when she walked in and circled Scara in a purring fit. Rosalie, Scara's mother, held the door open.

"She misses her mama already," Rosalie said and kissed Scara on both cheeks. "Your sister is cooking up a storm in the kitchen."

"Oh, I can smell it. Her lasagna is even better than yours," Scara said.

"You don't have to tell me that, I'm more than happy to let her go in the kitchen. She cooks circles around all of us. I don't know why she decided to sell houses instead."

"I do, she's pretty and makes a shit ton more selling houses. She's smart because when she gets older, she can fall back on this cooking stuff."

"I heard that," Lisa said. She stepped into the living room and Scara immediately gave her a hard hug.

"Hey, I missed you too, you trying to pop my eyes out?" Lisa asked and kissed her sister on the cheek.

"I'm sorry. I'm overdoing it, aren't I?" Scara asked. Tears were filling her eyes. She took a second when she backed away from Lisa and absorbed her surroundings. Her mother's house hadn't changed very much over the years. The same pictures lined the walls; the same carpet was on the floor; the same furniture was in the living room. She could almost smell her father's cigars. Joey's smile crept into her mind and Scara couldn't help but tear up. The nostalgia of this home washed over her and it woke up suppressed emotions from her youth. She always loved this house in Decatur. It was close enough to the city to go anywhere they needed but far enough out to get away from the onslaught of the Atlanta population. Their father had been dead for a good dozen years and Lisa felt the emotion transfer to her from Scara and her eyes welled up too. Rosalie was just happy to see her only two daughters in the same room together. Joey ran through her mind and she smiled, thinking that he was with them in some way. This was a rare occurrence, indeed.

"How you holding up?" Lisa asked as she motioned for them to move to the family kitchen and sit at the family table. Scara and Rosalie followed.

"Ok, I guess. I'm nervous about tomorrow. I have to be at the airport by 9:00 so I need to catch an Uber by 6:00 at the latest. You know how congested that airport can get," Scara said. Rosalie was stroking Scara's head like she used to when Scara was little. She was really taking advantage of the opportunity to live in the past if only for just a little while.

"Yeah, I hate our airport. Every connecting flight in the universe seems to come through Atlanta. I mean, how can that be, really? We're a tiny blip on the east coast but if you judged by our airport, we are the centerpiece for world travel. You can't get

anywhere quickly in that airport, that's for sure. And the people…
don't get me started. Most of them aren't from around here and are
rude as shit. Sorry for the language, Mom." Lisa smiled in her
mother's direction and she got one right back.

"Well, I have an almost nine hour flight to Edinburgh," Scara
said.

"Well, if you think about it, that's not so bad. Not bad at all,
actually. What's the time difference between here and Edinburgh?"

"They are five hours ahead of us."

"That's not that bad either. I mean California is three hours
behind us so five hours ahead of us ain't that much of a difference
if you really think about it. Yeah, it'll be an adjustment but just
don't nap on the plane and go to bed a little early for their time
when you get there and you should adjust pretty quickly."

"Maybe, it might take me a couple of days to adjust…strange
bed, strange place and all."

"Did you get through to Jeff today? Lisa asked and knew the
answer immediately by Scara's facial expression.

"No, I don't know if he's gotten into some trouble or
something. I missed a call the other day and could kick myself for
it but nothing since. I meant to mail a letter to him yesterday letting
him know if there is an emergency and he needs to get a hold of
me that he needs to call you. I'll give it to you before I leave if you
can mail it for me."

"You know I will. I like Jeff. It's just fuc… I mean messed up that he got in that mess. He's a good dude and I know that you love him. Just a tragedy," Lisa finished.

"Can we talk about something else?" Rosalie interrupted.

"Yeah, Mom, what do you want to talk about?" Scara looked at Rosalie.

"I want to talk about what time we are going to eat, I'm starving. It's torture smelling that lasagna and garlic bread."

"My garlic bread! Oh shit!" Lisa shouted and rushed to open the oven. She pulled the over-sized oven mitt from the hook and removed the pan with the garlic bread. It was just beginning to teeter from brown to burnt but Lisa caught it in time thanks to her mother's interjection.

"Ok, the bread was all I was really waiting on. Scara put the salad bowl on the table."

"Yes, ma'am," Scara said as she grabbed the large bowl filled with lettuce, tomatoes, onions, croutons and cucumbers. The shredded cheese was on the table along with the plates and cutlery.

"Mama, Sheena hasn't been a problem, has she?"

"No, she hasn't. You might not get her back when you return," Rosalie said with a smile.

"She might not want to come home with me when I come back, seems she's already acclimated to her new surroundings."

"Ok, everybody, dig in." Lisa walked in with the piping hot pan of lasagna. The women took from the bowl and then the lasagna pan.

"So, what's the best way to stay in touch with you while you are in Scotland?" Rosalie asked.

"Facebook messenger, I would say. So Mama that means you need to login and make sure the Facebook account Lisa set up for you a while back still works. You need to do that before I leave tonight."

"It's still active. I log into it once a week under Mama's profile just to make sure it's active. Mama, I'll show you how to get into it again before Scara leaves."

"Thank you, Lisa. I never got into the social media craze. I saw someone on Good Morning America the other day, pretty young girl, and her job was being a social media influencer. What the hell is that all about? It sounded to me like she just spouts off whatever is on her mind while on her phone and people pay her to do that. Please tell me that there is more to it than that," Rosalie said and grabbed a piece of garlic bread.

"Unfortunately, Mama, that is pretty much exactly how it works," Scara said.

"Well, I could do that job. You want to set me up on Facebook to be a social media influencer?" Rosalie asked and her daughters laughed. That brought a smile to Rosalie's face. It had been a while since her girls were in the same room together with her and even longer since they shared a laugh. Joey was always good at getting them to laugh.

"I'm sure you would make a fine social media influencer, Mama. Scara, I looked up the High Street hotel, looks nice. I wish

I could take some time off to join you but the market is ripe and I'm absolutely swamped with all of these houses. Rates have never been lower and that means I've never been busier," Lisa said.

"It's ok; I think I needed to do this on my own. My own, '*search for self*' quest is what I'm calling it," Scara said and took her first bite of lasagna. "Oh my God, Lisa! I actually forgot how good this was," Scara said.

"I don't know who taught you how to make your lasagna this way, I know it wasn't me, but whoever it was, you need to marry them," Rosalie said after she swallowed her first bite.

"Ok, here's the lowdown. Edinburgh is five hours ahead of us, Mama so I'll make sure to message you at a decent hour, not past your bedtime. I'm not sure how busy my first week will be. I know there are some local festivities that Jeff wanted to surprise me with but I'll play it by ear when I get there. I'm sure..." Scara began but her cell phone started buzzing. It caught her off guard because nobody had called her lately. She hadn't even gotten any calls from anyone telling her that she needed to extend her car's warranty. Before all the shit happened, Scara enjoyed getting those calls. She enjoyed screwing with the call center employee on the other end. She looked at the phone and it read: Unknown Caller, so she let it buzz until it stopped. She started to speak and it immediately began buzzing again, still the Unknown Caller. This time she took it.

"Hello."

"Hello, Kira."

"Jeff?" Scara asked already knowing it wasn't her husband. He was the only one that ever called her that.

"You know it's not Jeff. I'm just calling to wish you safe travels," said the disguised voice. It was distorted and very low. It was meant to sound like a man but it could have been either a man or woman.

"Melissa?"

"Just be careful, Kira. Local legends have a way of getting into the superstitious minds of outsiders." The call was disconnected.

"Was that Jeff?" Rosalie asked, showing concern because of the look on Scara's face.

Scara nodded. "It was nobody."

Rosalie and Lisa both knew that was a lie but they finished their dinner together in an uncomfortable silence. It was always the silence. The silence that kept creeping back up on Scara like a lost puppy dog that refused to stay lost.

CHAPTER 14

August 7, 2020: 2:22 PM – Edinburgh Airport

Claire Giblet was anxiously waiting for Delta Flight A8914 from Atlanta, GA to arrive. It was almost 2:30 PM. Claire held a sign that read **M. RUSHING**. They had corresponded over the last couple of weeks regarding the Ferry Fair and Melissa had sent her early drafts of the thesis she was working on. When Claire looked at Melissa's Facebook profile she was, like most folks that first saw her, struck by her natural beauty. There was very little or no make up in most of Melissa's pictures. Claire figured she should be easy to spot in the approaching group but she let the thought run through her brain that maybe she was being cat-fished but didn't put much credence in it. She supposed that a really dedicated catfish would go so far as to get a few thousand words into a thesis to keep up the charade but that would move them from catfish to psychotic in Claire's mind.

Melissa saw Claire first. Melissa's first thought was that Claire was cute as a button. She was standing there holding a cardboard sign with Melissa's name written carefully in bold black Sharpie letters. Claire was a little taller than Melissa thought and her hair was a darker shade of brown than what she saw in Claire's Facebook profile so Claire obviously visited hair salons or colored her own hair; either way she knew that Claire's hair was subject to a color change every now and again. Melissa waved to get Claire's attention and hollered out, "Claire! Hey!"

Claire's face lit up when she saw her and began waving her arm back and forth vigorously like Forrest Gump waving to Lieutenant Dan.

"Melissa! Hello!" Claire was beaming. Melissa moved a little faster. She stopped in front of Claire, let go of the luggage and gave her a big hug.

"Oh, Claire, it's so nice to finally meet you in person. You've been such a help to me," Melissa said as she stepped back. She looked up at Claire.

"Melissa, the feeling is mutual. I am so happy you chose South Queensferry and the Ferry Fair as your topic. What you've written so far is brilliant. It truly is but I think now that you're here and can experience the festivities for yourself, you will see how much better it can be, but let me stop myself before I break into a nonstop chatterbox in the middle of the airport. I'm sure you have a bag or two to retrieve." Claire was smiling so hard that Melissa thought that her teeth may shatter.

"I do have one big bag to grab and the other one I rolled right along with me," Melissa said.

"Well, let's stroll on over to baggage claim, shall we?"

"We shall," Melissa answered. Again, she felt deja vu with how quickly she was taking to Claire. The last time she took to a woman so quickly, it didn't work out so well. So much so, that was the sole reason she was here. She wasn't all that down with forgive and forget when she was forgotten in the middle of the fucking lake. She pushed those memories back and kept the smile on her face all the way through baggage claim and into the parking lot.

"I'll pop the trunk real quick," said Claire. Melissa was confused for just a second when Claire opened what would have been the passenger side door if they were in the United States but Melissa reminded herself that this wasn't Augusta, Georgia anymore. Claire helped Melissa heave the larger bag into the trunk of the older model Nissan Maxima, it looked like it had lived a long life and Melissa was surprised to hear the engine purr like a kitten when Claire started her up. She was older but she was well taken care of mechanically, that was for sure.

"Ok, so first things first, I'll take you to the hotel so you can settle in. I think you'll only be there for the two nights you booked. You can just stay with me the rest of the time. I have an apartment three blocks away from where you are staying," Claire jumped right into the conversation.

"That sounds good. I wish I could just cancel the two nights I've paid for. I'd love to talk to you deep into the night tonight," Melissa said.

"You want me to stay with you at the hotel? I don't mind, it's not much of a walk," Claire said.

Melissa backtracked a little bit, "I'd love that but I may have spoken too soon for my body. Let's have a bite of dinner and we can continue our discussion but I may turn in early tonight for our big day tomorrow," Melissa said.

"That makes perfect sense, perfect sense. Let's get you there so you can settle in. I can swing by and we can walk to dinner. There are a number of restaurants close by to choose from. My treat on your first night and I won't hear any argument about it," Claire said.

"No argument," Melissa replied.

"That's the right attitude. Tomorrow is the day before the Burryman march begins. From your paper, tell me what you remember about South Queensferry," Claire asked.

"I didn't know there was going to be a pop quiz," Melissa replied.

"Oh, you don't have to answer if you can't remember..."

"I didn't say that, I said I didn't know there was going to be a pop quiz but from what I recall during research is that South Queensferry was once a small fishing village and way back in the thirteenth century, it became what you call a Burgh. I'd call them towns but anyway the purpose was for businesses to start up and for people to make money. There was this guy, he was The Abbot of...shit...," Melissa said as she struggled to recall the name.

"No, he wasn't The Abbot of Shit, he was the Abbot of Dumfermline," Claire helped.

"Yeah, I knew it started with a D. Anyway, he had jurisdiction over the territory; he kept some trade money on merchandise exported from his jurisdiction and money on the imports that came from the crown. King Robert, if I recall correctly. And to expand the Burgh was granted the right to hold a weekly market and an annual fair. This was the real start of the Ferry Fair."

"Very good, Melissa, very good but, there is another belief that is not covered in your paper," Claire said.

"Really? What would that be?"

"Some believe that the weekly fair started even before the thirteenth century. As far back as 1068, in the time of King Malcolm III and his Queen, and it were her visits to Dunfermline Abbey on a ferry boat that gave us the name of our town. It was actually a civic duty to walk the boundaries of Queensferry, which were always guarded. Now, over time it became a social duty to celebrate the day with food, drink and dancing. This was the true beginning of the Ferry Fair. At least that is what a lot of us Scots believe, myself included."

"Wow," Melissa replied. "I wished I would have recorded everything you just said."

"It's not like you can't write it down. You'll have me for the next seven days."

"So, what is tomorrow's agenda?" Melissa asked.

"Well, the Ferry Fair won't actually start until Saturday. Tomorrow is Thursday so I figured you might need some adjustment time and Friday is the march of the Burryman."

"Stag Head hotel is where it starts that morning and ends there in the evening."

"That's right. So, tomorrow is your call. I can pick you up around midday tomorrow and take you to lunch and show you around Queensferry if you would like."

"That sounds like a plan, Stan," Melissa replied.

"Stan?"

"Just an expression, sounds great."

CHAPTER 15

August 8, 2020: 9:00 AM – South Queensferry

Preparations were well underway for the upcoming Burryman festival and Ferry Fair. Andrew Maddaford was brushing at his new kilt. The alterations were just finished at Stewart Christie & Co. Andrew could tell as soon as he pulled the newly fitted kilt around his waist that it was money well spent. He could have gotten one at the shop in which he was employed but kilts from Stewart Christie & Co are top of the line; the best of the best. Andrew smiled and bent at the knees – arms outstretched. He felt a pulse of energy shoot through his body. It had been a while since he felt energized. He was mentally exhausted for sure and physically, he wasn't quite there but he could feel that it wasn't far off. But today, when he wrapped the kilt around his stocky frame, it put some come along in his giddy up. He felt strong. He would need his strength. This would be his first year of what he hoped were many of donning the costume of the Burryman. He was looking forward to it.

Nine hours later.

Andrew Maddaford was in the closing minutes of his shift at Scotland Shoppe on Queensferry Street when he surprisingly found himself in the midst of a conversation with a beautiful young woman.

"The Burryman brings us good luck and fortune," Andrew said to Scara. "And this year, I have been selected to be the Burryman. It is quite an honor."

"What do you do as the Berry Man?" Scara asked. She purposely asked the question that way to seem like a wide eyed tourist.

"No, not berry man, Burryman; we don't do anything with berries, Mrs. Slayfield."

"Scara, just call me Scara."

"Ok, Scara. The Burryman is a very old tradition of ours. So far back that I don't rightly know when it truly began. I suppose I could Google it and it would tell me some things that I don't already know but I know that it's been happening long before I came along and I reckon it will still be going long after we're both dead and gone. The second Friday of August every year is when the Burryman starts his walk. I'll put on a suit of burrs, flowers and ferns just like the many men before me and walk through South Queensferry drinking whisky and collecting coin. I'll do this for nine hours, that is, if I don't fall down drunk from all of the whisky. And many of the folks will bring their very own burrs to stick on me; it will bring them luck and good fortune. It's a tremendous honor to be selected."

"Sounds like it," Scara said. She moved closer to Andrew and he seemed to flinch just a bit, not sure of what this gorgeous woman was about to do. She moved past him and walked to the front of the shop. "What time will you start your march tomorrow?"

"Well, I'll be at the Stag Head at 7:00 AM where George O'Hare and some other blokes will begin burring me up so to speak. I'll start about quarter till nine and go until six o'clock unless I'm comatose by then."

"That's going to be a very long day for you. Can I see your costume?"

"I'll do you one better, would you like to assist me throughout the day tomorrow? I'll need two people to help me hold the staves and a couple of bell-ringers. Do you think you might want to be one of my assistants? You'll get an up close view of Queensferry, that's for sure. You'll be a part of something truly unique to our community," Andrew finished convincingly.

Scara took a second to think about the proposition of the burly redheaded man. He was a handsome Scottish lad for sure and she felt ashamed at the attraction.

"I think that would be a great time. I would love to do that. What, what are you doing now? I'm sorry to be so forward but I don't really know anyone here, well, besides you now, and I want to know where I could grab a bite. I haven't had anything filling since last night."

"Well, if you can hang tight for another twenty minutes, I'll be off from my shift and we can walk over to The Boathouse. You will love it if you like seafood."

"I love seafood and that sounds amazing. Thank you, Andrew."

"I should be thanking you, I mean a beautiful woman like yourself being seen in public with me," Andrew said with a self deprecating grin.

"I do think you're rather handsome, Andrew, but you do see the ring on my left hand don't you?"

"I do, but I'm not a prier, I'm a mind my own business kind of guy."

"That's good, Andrew, I'm so glad to hear that because I'm not into answering a lot of personal questions."

"I'll get only what you share."

"Ok, then, I can wait twenty minutes."

Andrew smiled and looked at the clock, "Well, now you only have to wait fifteen."

———

Twenty four minutes later. The Boathouse.

"Scara, I think we should start with the grilled goats' cheese on pave risotto with caramelized red onion and redcurrant jelly. What do you think?"

"I think that sounds disgusting and delicious at the same time," Scara replied. She felt the little gnaw of guilt but shut it down; this wasn't a date. Andrew wasn't a date. She loved her husband.

"What's disgusting about it?" Andrew asked.

"Goats' cheese, I've never had it."

"I know they have goats' cheese in the states," Andrew returned.

"Yep, and I've never had it there either."

"Well, if you've never had it, how do you know it's disgusting? You will love it, I promise. Just be willing to let your palate explore," Andrew said with an impish grin.

"Ok, what about the main course?" Scara asked as she scanned the menu and continued, "How about the hot seafood platter? King prawns, you know I didn't know what a prawn was until Jeff had to explain it to me, a *fancy word for shrimp* is what he said. The platter has mussels, soft shell crab, queenie scallops, squid served with garlic hollandaise and fries. I don't know about the squid but I do love fries and that's as American as you can get," Scara said.

"Well since fries came from Belgium, I don't see how that is as American as you can get but let's just go with it," Andrew said as he waved over the pretty, fair haired waitress.

Andrew ordered the appetizer and entrée before the two continued their conversation.

"So, Andrew, I'm pretty stoked about our Burryman day. I can't wait to see the costume. Where can I get some burrs of my own to stick on it?"

"Oh, I think we can, how do you say it in the United States, round up burrs from somewhere."

"Round up, huh? That's actually a weed killer in America so you don't want any part of Round Up if you're going to essentially be a walking weed."

"Well, I could be smoking weed," Andrew replied. He was on fire tonight; or so he thought.

"Well, I won't be doing any of that," Scara's smile faded.

"Hey, what did I say? No gloom faces here."

"I can't help it, I'm thinking of the man I love. Oh shit, I'm starting to sound like a fucking Hallmark movie and I definitely ain't a Hallmark kind of girl."

"What is a Hallmark movie? Should I be familiar?"

"It's nothing and no, no you really shouldn't. Not if you want to keep your man card."

"Man card? Don't know what that means but ok, I'm not a prier," Andrew said smiling.

"And, I'm not a crier," Scara replied, a grin snaked across her lips.

"I'm a listener but I'm not a prier," Andrew repeated.

"I'm normally not a spiller but I'll probably never see you again when I leave, so I think I do want to do something out of character and spill some things."

The waitress approached with their appetizers and Scara smiled at her. She set the tray of food in between the two of them and refilled their drinks before asking if they needed anything else. Andrew politely said no and Scara continued.

"I married the love of my life and he's in prison for something that I did."

"Get out of here," Andrew whispered, trying to figure out if there was jest in the statement, but found none and got quiet as he grabbed a bite of goats' cheese.

"I shot and killed a man. Well, for all intents and purposes, I killed a man and my husband took the fall for me. He was protecting me and I feel so guilty just being here. For…just sitting here…just talking to you and…"

"And…what?"

"Feeling attracted to a stranger in Scotland. It feels like one of those fucking Hallmark movies."

"I'd lose my man card."

"You would, you would lose your man card," Scara smiled as she put a piece of goats'' cheese into her mouth and the flavor exploded in her palate. "Wow, this is really good, and it came from a goat?"

"What is his name?" Andrew asked, breaking the light banter.

"Jeff," Scara was surprised with the ease that she blurted out the answer on command. "And the man you killed?"

"Ronald."

"Did he have it coming?" Andrew asked.

"He did not. It was a horrific accident," Scara replied.

"And your husband… is he the jealous type?" Andrew asked as his eyes narrowed their focus onto Scara's.

"He is," she replied with a nervous grin and was about to ask him what his definition of not being a prier was but she let it go because Andrew's face brightened up which signaled he had let it go.

"Well, then let's not do anything to get him angry," Andrew said.

Scara's tension eased and the fair haired cutie walked up with their main course.

CHAPTER 16

August 9, 2020, 7:00 AM – South Queensferry

Andrew was steadying his breath as he was becoming familiar with the suit of burrs. He was covered with nature's Velcro. Scara was fascinated with the precision in which the old man was applying the burrs. From the bottom of his feet to the top of his head, Andrew was being covered with the green brown patches. His arms were stuck stiffly out to his sides as if he were Jesus assuming his position on the cross. The suit allowed very little in the way of flexibility. The old man wasn't the only person helping Andrew with his suit, there were four other much younger men placing burrs all over Andrew.

"What are the burrs, exactly?" Scara curiously asked.

"They are pestilential sticky seed-heads of Burdock," said the elderly man applying them to the suit fabric attached to Andrew.

"Pesti whatseewhoseit?" Scara replied, smiling.

"Pestilential sticky seed-heads of Burdock, my dear," the elderly man turned and saw her beautiful face for the first time which put a smile on his own wrinkled mug. "Well, hello, my name is George O'Hare." He stood and held out a hand. Scara took it and he gave hers a quick kiss. His thick white mustache tickled the top of her hand.

"Seed-heads got it. They are so prickly, huh?"

"That they are, our young Andrew here is going to have a long day today."

"Well, so am I then. I'm supposed to help him today. I will be accompanying him on his trek. Andrew told me a little about the Burryman last night but I'm curious by nature, what can you tell me about the Burryman?" Scara asked certain that the old timer would give a more detailed answer than the young man being suited up… and she would be right.

"Well, the legend of the Burryman goes back centuries," George began as he continued to place the burrs upon the costumed man. "It was much more widespread in years long gone by but as it has died down in other parts of Scotland, we have kept it alive and well here in South Queensferry. When I say years long gone by, I'm talking hundreds of years, young lady. You see what was called the Ferry Fair was started by George II in 1687 and has long since given way to a simple gala where we will have a Ferry Queen. We will have what we call a burgh race where someone will win a pair of boots that will be delivered by a halberd."

"What's a halberd?" Scara asked. She was sucked into the history lesson now.

"A weapon my dear. Think of it like a spear with an axe attached to the pointy end. An effective close combat weapon back in its time for sure. Then there are the seemingly endless shows and social gatherings. Actually the Burryman walk used to take place in July and not August. I expect it was changed to August so the burrs could ripen and be as, how do you say it, prickly as possible. As far as our lad Andrew here, or more directly, the legend of the Burryman, there are a number of interpretations. I can name a couple if you aren't weary of my rambling."

"Please do, I find it all fascinating," Scara replied.

"Well, the actual root meaning of the ceremony has been debated for centuries and the interpretations have changed over time to where we are today. The concept was that the people are seeking good fortune for the town or harvest wherever the ceremony is performed. The harvest could possibly be bounty from the sea. Buckie and Fraserburgh once had their own Burrymen. In Buckie, if the fishing was bad or if the bounty wasn't very good, they used to have a cooper dressed from head to toe in burrs placed in a barrow and wheeled through the town in hopes of turning the fortune of the bounty around. In Fraserburgh, the Burryman would ride in on horseback, imagine that, riding horseback covered in these blessed things," George smiled as he lifted a burr patch to his face. "Same purpose, to bring good fortune and harvest and, if I remember my lessons correctly, the ritual in Fraserburgh ended in 1867. One of the more unpopular origins of the Burryman would lead us to believe that he is actually a scapegoat. A collector of all of the guilt built up in the village. He would take it all away to wash the villagers clean; remind you of anyone in Christianity?" George grinned as he asked the question and continued. "He would collect the villagers' sins and be drove out at the end of the day. This is one most folks shun; most folks don't like this interpretation of the legend. Me, I'm not so sure that wasn't the original intent all along. Burr him up, scar him up, put it all on the

Burryman and let him wipe the slates clean so we can all dirty them up again. Really, does it sound like a certain man in Christianity that hung on a cross?" George asked again, being very blunt this time.

"George, you have managed to bring the room down with the last interpretation," Andrew mumbled from under his balaclava hood. "George, it will be you, Scara and a few of the boys with me today. You feel up to walking around town with us all day and keeping me from crashing onto my face when I drink all of this whisky?"

"Well, this young lady has breathed another twenty years into my life by just looking at me so I'm sure that I can make it through the day with the two of you as long as she is close by."

"I'll be with both of you all day. I wanted the full experience and from the looks of it, that's exactly what I'm going to get."

"That's great to hear my dear, great to hear. You know, when we get up to leave, our lad Andrew here cannot utter another word until the day is done. He will drink and collect burrs and coins," George said and looked directly into Scara's brown eyes. His were green pools and she felt her heart flutter a little. George' skin may have aged but there was still quite the twinkle in his eyes.

"That suit looks rather...cumbersome," Scara began and George was already anticipating the next question but let her ask it anyway. "How, how is he supposed to go to the bathroom?"

"Well, he can't my dear. There are no easy openings in this costume. We're going to have to remove it piece by piece at the end of the day, much like we're putting it on piece by piece."

"And what are staves exactly? Andrew said that we would help him hold his staves."

George smiled and pointed at two colorful, flower covered staffs stacked beside each other in the corner of the room. "Those are staves, my dear, and he is going to have one fun time holding those out straight with both of his arms. It's impossible, really. Normally, this task is assigned to two men but Andrew here made it his mission to make sure that you were the second hand on his walk today. We do have the boys if they need to step in at any point."

Andrew was nodding his covered face in agreement.

"Can, can he breathe in that thing?" Scara asked.

"Of course he can breathe in it but he can't see very well. Another reason he needs the two of us, to help guide him so he doesn't get hurt walking about with those narrow eye slits. We will leave the Stag Head at eight forty five sharp to start our journey and head over for his first drink at the Provost's house. We will walk the whole South Queensferry and the Burryman will receive the whisky and burrs bringing good luck to everyone he meets."

CHAPTER 17

August 9, 2020: 8:42 AM – South Queensferry

The march of the Burryman was officially set to begin at 8:45 AM and Scara and George were standing to each side of Andrew. The young men had done their jobs well and Scara couldn't comprehend how Andrew could stand in such a suit. He was completely unrecognizable; fully covered from head to foot in burrs.

"You know, in some tales of Burryman lore, there was a Queen that walked with the Burryman. People may think we are bringing that back since you are joining the march today. You're pretty enough to be a Queen, that's for certain," George said. His charm was full on and Scara smiled at the old gentleman.

"These staves have some weight, don't they?" Scara directed her question to Andrew but George put a finger to his lips.

"The Burryman can't speak for the duration of this trip my lady, the fortune he brings will blow away if he utters a word."

"Oh, I'm sorry, I forgot. I hope he can see well enough. I can't even see his eyes."

"That's another thing, my dear. Don't try to look directly into his eyes, which is also considered bad luck. Our job is to walk the path with him, let him drink whisky, collect burrs, coins and get him back to the Stag Head at six o'clock, more or less. We can talk with the folks all we want, which is why I think Andrew thought this would be a good experience for an out-of-towner like you and

I agree with him. This should be the experience of a lifetime. Just listen to what people say to the Burryman. Listen to the requests and the sincerity in their tones. Some of the younger children get frightened by his appearance but the older ones actually run up to the Burryman and try to embrace him. Let's keep them at bay the best we can because he's going to get easier to tip over with the more whisky he drinks. We are going to have to keep the staves held up because it won't take long for his arms to tire. We will lead him from place to place and the bell-ringers will shout at each one, you can join in once you see how they are doing it. The residents will come out, give their greetings, place burrs on his costume and give coins that we will put back into the town."

"Wow, you're going to do all of that and not even keep the money, that sucks Burryman," Scara said to Andrew, careful to not look into his face – taking the old man's advice.

"It's almost quarter till, we need to make our way to the first stop. We will begin our walk to Villa Road and he will have his first whisky at the Provost's House. We need to be there at 9:00 AM, not a minute later. Let's get his flag wrapped around his waist and get the show on the road."

Scara smiled and repeated, "Let's get the show on the road."

"Off to Villa Road we go," George said and nodded toward Andrew. Scara stood on one side and George on the other as they left the Stag Head.

There were children everywhere when the group stepped outside.

"It's him! It's him!" one of the light haired boys was hollering. It was as if he saw a real life super hero come walking out to save the day. The two younger boys standing behind him were staring at the Burryman in their own trances – they were also enamored, like their older brother, with the green mass of man slowing moving their way.

"Ok, lads, get back now! You can put burrs on him at Provost, move on now!" George happily shouted. There was no hint of anger in his bellow, it was more of a jolly man urging the kids to go wait on their prize; it would be worth the wait. He gave that feeling of *don't approach Santa while he's under the tree*, you'll see him soon enough. The Burryman march was now officially underway. Children and parents weren't the only ones interested.

09:00 AM – The Provost's House

The line of folks at the Provost's House was long and growing. Andrew's vision was limited to front only through the narrow slits in his mask. Peripheral vision was out of the question. And, he couldn't utter a sound. He didn't have to urinate yet but the thought started dancing in his mind as he imagined the number of whisky shots he'd have to down on his journey. On the plus side, it was hot as Hades in this plant suit so he was pretty sure he would sweat off a lot more than he could piss out. His bladder may just catch a break. He had a good number two early in the morning well before George and the young men showed up to start burring him up. As for smell, all Andrew could really smell were the sickly

131

sweet scents of the flowers that were placed all over the burs. He wished that he could get a good whiff of Scara's scent. Whatever perfume she was wearing the night before left a longing in his nostrils for more. Jane McCaskle was the first one to hold whisky to his lips. She was a short lady and a little on the heavy side. Scara had to help guide the straw into the narrow opening where Andrew's lips could feel it.

"This is for you, thank you for bringing favor and prosperity to Queensferry," Jane blushed when she felt the Burryman pull the whisky into his mouth. She felt a rush of honor and bashfulness hit her at the same time.

Jane pulled the glass away from the Burryman's mouth. The three light haired brothers had hands full of burrs and were excited to plop them onto the Burryman's midsection. The youngest one, Scott Dougal had the widest eyes of the three of them.

"Burrah Man! Burrah Man!" the four year old Scott screamed happily as he pushed burr upon burr onto the Burryman's stomach.

"It's Burryman!" the oldest brother Ridley (he was a ripe old seven), corrected. "The Burryman will take out all of the bad guys! He will protect us all! When I get bigger, I want to be the Burryman!"

This made Andrew smile underneath the hot mask; he remembered his own excitement as a child at one day being the Burryman and, here he was, doing it. The children mimicking him warmed his heart.

Another man approached with whisky in hand, it was Timmy Sullivan, local bar owner and he knew how to have a good time. "You look thirsty, Burryman! Drink up! Be careful, this has some hop!" He shoved the straw into the mouth opening like he was filling up a tank of gas and Andrew tried to move his arms out in front of himself on instinct but the costume wouldn't let him stretch them very far. His only recourse was to chomp down on the straw before he drank down the burning whisky.

Scara looked at the faces of the townsfolk; they were happy, truly happy. It was a look that she longed for when she saw herself in the mirror. And she remembered the sign she first noticed when she set eyes on the town of Queensferry. It was the arms of the burgh and there was something about the figure on the insignia that made Scara feel as if she belonged here. A figure of hope standing crowned on a vessel with his scepter in one hand and his bible in the other. She wasn't sure who the figure was supposed to be, but looking at him gave Scara a feeling of comfort when she took the short ten mile ride from Edinburgh to the Ferry.

———————

09:20 AM: Farguhar Terrace

The Burryman, George and Scara made it to Farguhar Terrace per the schedule and Scara fell in love with the exterior of the fine homes that lined the street. They were connectors, one home connected to another as if they were brothers and sisters of the same brick-master. They had the look of age and character. Some of the houses looked like they would invite you in for a rest if they could talk. Everything here was so warm, so inviting, and so lovely.

At the corner of 25 Farquhar Terrace was a smiling boy. He was grinning from ear to ear. He had dark hair and even darker eyes. The boy was wearing some sort of coveralls, maybe corduroy from what Scara could see. He started moving toward them and the closer he got, Scara could make out more of his features. He was young, that was for sure, but there was something in his face that was hardened. His teeth were a jangled mess of crookedness when he revealed them, erasing his closed lipped grin. He looked rather strange to Scara and this boy was the first thing bordering on unpleasant that she had seen since setting foot in the Ferry. And, she felt ashamed for allowing herself to have such a thought. She forced a smile to the young man as he held out his hand.

"It's for him," the young man said with a squeaky voice and held his closed fist out to Scara. She stole a glance over to George and he nodded to let her know that it was ok. She could accept the gift on behalf of the Burryman. Scara opened her palm and the boy dropped the coin into it.

"Thank you," Scara replied and George nodded his approval.

"Oh, it's just a pittance," the young man replied. He didn't say it in a way that conveyed embarrassment; it was more matter of fact.

"I'm sure the Burryman will show favor upon you and your family, my boy," George cut in.

"I don't have a family, sir. I am on my own," the young man stated once again matter-of-factly.

"That can't be," Scara began, "you can't be any older than eleven."

"I'm aged fourteen years if you must know," he replied.

"What's your name?" Scara asked. She was really ashamed of her first impression of this homeless kid.

"Doesn't matter what my name is; the only thing that really matters is what you did," the boy said and his jagged tooth mouth may as well have spit razors in Scara's face.

"What, what did you just say?" Scara asked and before she could get any more words out, the boy dropped back and disappeared into the crowd of folks. Scara's stomach was in knots and she desperately wanted one of those whisky shots.

CHAPTER 18

August 9, 2020: 9:40 AM – Springfield View

The bell-ringers, Cameron and Seth, followed behind Scara and George on the march. They rang the bells and shouted the Burryman's appearance in one accord, "HIP, HIP HOORAY! IT'S THE BURRYMAN'S DAY!" Scara was taking it all in. She thought of the jagged toothed homeless boy that approached a couple of stops back; she let her mind begin to believe that he never really existed. She justified that it was the noises and chatter of all of the folks that wanted to gain favor with the Burryman that conjured up the *snaggle toothed boy of guilt.*

The people on Springfield View congregated around one of the flats at the front end of the street. They were excited by the bell-ringers with their announcement of the Burryman's arrival. George was steadying Andrew's right hand on the stave and Scara was attentive and doing the same on the left side. Scara saw the little woman with the cup of whisky approach and she wanted to take one for the team and drink that down but, not her land, not her rules. George grabbed the cup from the old lady and guided the plastic cup sans straw into the opening and the old lady was happy when she heard gulps as whisky was being swallowed by the Burryman. She would have good fortune this year; she had done her part. Behind her was a child with a handful of burrs. The Burryman's costume would just about double in burrs by the time the day's journey was over. Kids, especially, loved to plop them on by the handfuls. The dang things just stuck to one another so easily. The Burryman would look like a geographical map at the end of the day – burr-mountains spread all over his body.

Scara smiled at the little girl and the little girl smiled back at her. The smile made Scara gasp. The little girl had the same jagged toothed grin as the homeless boy.

"Scara, you won't escape what you did. The Burryman will show you no favor. You can't make amends," the little girl said. Scara was sure that she had to be hallucinating. The little girl had blonde curls and the deepest blue eyes that she had ever seen; you could almost dive into them. And she wasn't dressed in scraps like the homeless boy; this girl had on a new red, checkered dress and fancy shoes. Her grin was the same though, jagged and menacing. Scara turned toward George who was helping the Burryman keep his arm steady. He paid no attention to the little girl. Scara turned back to the girl but, just like that, she was gone. She wasn't in the crowd and Scara was afraid her dream was finally coming to take her. Something didn't feel right here. She would have to continue the march of the Burryman, she didn't have a choice. Cameron and Seth boomed behind her, "HIP, HIP HOORAY! IT'S THE BURRYMAN'S DAY!"

So, it was time to ease on down the road. The thought rolled in Scara's brain as they kept marching, *The Burryman will show you no favor. You can't make amends.* Scara knew that was a true sentiment, she couldn't make amends for the things she had done. The Burryman would show her no favor. Scara, in this moment, as they moved from Springfield View and onto Springfield Road, wished that she had cancelled this trip. The silence was coming.

CHAPTER 19

August 9, 2020: 10:50 AM – Station Road

The march continued.

"HIP, HIP HOORAY! IT'S THE BURRYMAN'S DAY!"

There was flat after flat lined up and down Station Road. Scara's heart was racing. There was no sign of the snaggled tooth boy or girl.

"You ok, dear?" George noticed Scara's hand shaking as she was supporting the Burryman's arm – the stave in his left hand looked as if it may slip out at any moment.

"I'm fine, just taking it all in," Scara tried to paint on a grin but George could see her frantic eyes tattling on her.

"One of the boys can relieve you, I insist," George said and raised a hand to Cameron, one of the bellowing bell-ringers. The tall man rushed to Scara's side and she relinquished the Burryman's support to Cameron. He smiled and offered Scara the bell. Scara took it but held it to her side. She would need to compose herself before she joined Seth in ringing and singing. Scara found herself staring at the back of the Burryman's head; it was turning into a jungle of guilt.

They were at a standstill as the Burryman sipped more whisky. The houses on Station Road were beautiful, many of them made of solid brick and standing two stories. Some had tall wooden fences that were stained to perfection while others had grand walkways to their entrances. A portly man stumbled closer to the Burryman with a handful of burrs. Scara raised her hand to ring the bell and the man stopped in front of her. His forehead was lathered in sweat and his eyes squinted at her as if he were trying to figure out if he'd known her. The man was as bald as the day he came into the world. Scara lowered the bell back to her side and she stared at the man squinting her down. He opened his mouth and Scara was shocked back into the world she was in. The man had the same snaggle toothed grin as the children she had already encountered.

"Your sins run deep, Scara. The silence is coming to claim you. The silence is coming to collect your debt," he said as he passed her by and placed his handful of burrs onto the Burryman's shoulder.

"What debt?" Scara asked. The man grinned at her once more before dropping back into the crowd.

———————

August 9, 2020: 11:40 AM – Rosebery Avenue

Scara wanted to quit. She wanted to call it a day and head back to the High Street hotel and just lay in the bed for the rest of her time in Queensferry. She was ringing the bell and mouthing the words to the increasingly mindless chant, "HIP, HIP HOORAY! IT'S THE BURRYMAN'S DAY!"

The people were cheering along. The townsfolk were lined up and down Rosebery Avenue. The Burryman lumbered forward. Scara moved in time as she raised and lowered the bell, sending dull clangs into the air with every swing. She felt a tug on her shirt and turned around and her mind tricked her into seeing the upturned grin of Johnny Pickens. She stumbled forward and almost dropped the bell before recovering. Watching her stumble, you would have thought she was the one drinking whisky at every stop. Andrew could never really see her as the mask forced his gaze forward. She looked back and Johnny's face was replaced by a little yapping dog. He had big floppy ears that were way too big for his face and his snout was long and narrow. He was a mix of quite a few breeds. Scara stopped ringing the bell and held her hand out to the pup's nose. He took a quick sniff and gave the top of her hand a lick. He pulled back and gave another quick yap before moving like an unseen master had just beckoned him to come quickly. Scara was feeling foolish. She was letting all of the shit that she had gone through finally come crashing into her and it was getting to her at the absolute worst time. She needed to fight through it and make the rest of this day about the Burryman and the fun all of the villagers were having in this tradition. She wanted to get into the spirit of the festivities and once again she had just about convinced herself that the snaggle-tooths were all figments of her overactive guilt. And, she was guilty.

A buxom woman that was maybe in her fifties was waiting at the end of the driveway of her home on Rosebery. She held the straw gently up to the mouth of the Burryman. Scara was relaxing now. She let herself smile at the woman and the woman smiled back. The smile made Scara's grin turn around and run in the opposite direction. It was the same snaggle toothed smile that Scara had seen enough of today.

"The Burryman will show no favor, you will bear the burden of the silence. It's coming for you, Scara. It's coming for you before the morning comes again," the chesty woman said before she left the sidewalk and walked back into her home. Scara had to keep ringing the bell. It was all set up for this she figured. She had plenty to atone for.

August 9, 2020: 1:00 PM – Wellhead Close

Scara was ringing and singing but at the same time thinking and reflecting on what she had learned about the Burryman's history from George in the brief time that he filled her in on the legend. Her mind kept going back to the word scapegoat. The words George spoke earlier came back to her with the clarity of reflection when you didn't quite understand it when first told – an *AHA* moment when something clicks in your head.

Wellhead Close was more of the same, burrs and whisky for the Burryman. If Scara had been in the moment, she would be amazed at Andrew's tolerance to keep marching and not puking his guts out inside that monstrosity of a costume that continued to grow at each stop.

The scapegoat take on the Burryman was gnawing at her. Scara was thinking of the silence. George had told her that Rene Girard (Scara had no clue who this person was but must be of some historical importance), thought that the practice of scape-goating could be seen from three separate lenses. One of them could be associated with some sort of community tragedy, emergency or crisis. Maybe a famine or flood or some other Universal act. Another could be the direct result of something more personal, something that could gnaw and break a person down. Something that they wanted to lay down at someone else's feet. Something that Scara did lay at someone else's feet. Something like murder. And the third thing that fit the criteria for a scapegoat that Rene Girard described in detail is when people have core differences that cannot be disquieted or when just live and let live was impossible. So much so, that it disrupts the community in such a profound way. And hadn't Scara experienced this as well.

Scara's mind was twisting around on the carousel. All of this was for the approaching silence.

There was another kid and another snaggle toothed grin. Another accusation spoken where only she could hear it. There was going to be a breaking point and it was fast approaching. Scara continued to ring, sing and smile. The next stop was Sommerville Gardens.

Sommerville Gardens had a number of flats for sale and Scara let herself, for a moment, imagine pulling up roots and living right here in Queensferry. She was just fantasizing, placing herself in a world where she could move willy nilly with no governing providence telling her where she belonged. The flats on Sommerville Gardens were neatly kept and many of the yard signs she noticed let her know that the majority of them were move in ready, right down to the washing machines and refrigerators. Scara imagined Jeff being here with her. The noise around her was becoming just that; noise. Scara was temporarily immersing herself; finding joy in the commitment of her mind. She filled her lungs with the extremely fresh air. She could feel the difference. The air in Atlanta, GA was filled with a lot of scents and many of them were the polar opposite of pleasant. Scara absentmindedly let the Burryman crew march on ahead of her as she pulled a flyer from the base of one of the signs advertising a flat for sale. This was a two bedroom terraced home and the description the flyer laid out made her want to live in her make believe world even more.

Scara read every word on the front of the flyer and stared carefully at every picture. The images fluttered through her mind like a silent movie. There she was, in black and white glory, walking through the new home, smiling every time she turned a door handle to walk into another room. She stepped into the kitchen and marveled at the marble counter tops and the checkered back splash behind the huge tub of a sink. The stainless steel refrigerator was dull against the stark light. She would get a fresh beer for Jeff. He would be home any minute. Scara felt as if she were walking on a cloud as she grabbed the cold handle and pulled the refrigerator door open. She stood, trembling. It got really cold and her eyes locked onto the darkness. There was nothing in the fridge. It was just a void; a portal to a star-less space. A silence fell over the room. The freezer door slowly opened like the lower half of a monster's jaws. It was also dark, silent and oh, so very cold. Scara's mouth was twitching. She was waiting for a ghostly hand to reach out and pull her into the silence. It was her time was all that she could think. It was her time to pay for the sins of her not too distant past. It wasn't a surprise to her at all. The joy she felt was ripped from her just like the shotgun blast that ripped through Ronald Simpkins' face.

"Scara, Mrs. Slayfield!" George exclaimed as he shook her by the arm. Scara dropped the flyer and she was back in the land of the Burryman's march.

"I'm sorry, George. I'm so sorry, I spaced out," Scara said as she trained a forced smile in the old man's direction; a forced smile that the old man did not buy.

"Do you need to go back to Stag Head? We have plenty of help here. You can go take a rest if you need it," George said and grabbed Scara by her hand. She looked directly into his face, trying to conceal the fear that was welling up. She didn't want him to open his mouth again. She didn't want to see a snaggle toothed grin spewing about the silence and how she wasn't going to get away from it. Scara didn't want to collapse in a psychotic episode in front of this man and her biggest fear in that moment was the fear of embarrassment. She didn't want to look like a looney bird in front of this man – this man who was easily forty years her senior and probably more. George, the man who knew the history of the Burryman better than the reigning Burryman himself. Maybe he took a turn at wearing the costume. Scara was pretty convinced that George had adorned the getup himself in the past and that was part of the reason for his passion. So, she didn't want to embarrass herself in front of this stranger that would never become a friend.

August 9, 2020: 2:15 PM – Scotstoun Avenue

The Burryman march continued into Scotstoun, an area that was established in the mid eighteen hundreds and used to adjoin shipyards. Now, many houses in Scotstoun are sought after because they retain features from a period long gone. Many have gardens that fit the mold of the West End.

Seth and Scara rang the bells. Scara felt as if she were at the epicenter of a storm. The smell of the greenery and colorful flowers around her made her feel somewhere between pleasant and sick. The odor was sweet but if she inhaled too deeply, it gave a push of nausea.

Andrew was wobbling along but he was still treading. He did release his bladder a couple of times during the day but nothing escaped the costume. It was so covered in burrs and the way he was lumbering along, poor Andrew looked like a sloshy swamp monster that if kicked in the back, would topple over and die flat on his face from hunger because he wouldn't be able to flip over and rise to his feet. Children still beckoned his name. One of those children grabbed Scara by her hand and tugged with authority.

"You're going to die in the silence," the little one said. Scara saw the snaggle toothed smile once more and replied, "Come on then, come on and let's get it over with." Then she kept marching.

CHAPTER 20

Bridges Pool Hall, 2:40 PM – South Queensferry

They had just arrived at Bridges Pool Hall. Scara got a much needed break and so did the Burryman. The owner of the bar held up a shot of Auchentoshan Malt Scotch whisky for the Burryman and Scara took a seat. The bar looked a little like home. There were a few billiard tables that lined the hardwood floor along with a dartboard that was in need of replacing because of the thousands upon thousands of piercings it had taken over the years yet it still stood like a warrior waiting for the next fight. Scara noticed the balding gentleman pointing the toy shotgun at the video screen of the arcade game against the wall. She heard the electronic crack of the shotgun and Scara jumped. The fake green shotgun shooting the digital shells took her back to their house. She blasted the hole through the door. Scara moved toward the man as he pumped the toy gun again and discharged. He registered her movement but paid her no mind as he continued to kill the zombie hoard moving his way. Scara could feel the silence taking over again. The man pulled back and cocked it again. Scara was close to him now. She looked over his right shoulder and had to suppress a scream. She was looking at her living room. Sheena was lying in her bed and she could see the barrel of the shotgun. It was out in front of her. She was now looking at her front door. The gun was cocked again, the shell loaded into the chamber. Scara reached for the barrel and jerked it away.

"Excuse me," the man said as he gave a startled look. He didn't get angry; he was more puzzled than anything else. "Do you want to play?" he asked. Scara was stuck there, not quite out of her episode and offered no reply.

"Miss, are you ok?" the stranger asked.

Scara looked back at the screen and she could see the blood dripping down with the words, YOU ARE DEAD, oozing down the center. The zombie hoard had overrun the poor soul that didn't fire his shotgun. Scara broke through the silence.

"Oh my, I'm so sorry, I don't know what has gotten into me," she said sheepishly.

She could hear the Burryman and crew off at the other side of the bar; he would be there another few minutes before they began the next phase of their trek.

"It's ok, you need a drink or is that the problem? You had too many?" the stranger asked. He grinned and Scara braced herself for the familiar snaggle toothed smile but there was none. His smile was white and bright.

"No, I think I'm still adjusting to the time difference and spaced out a bit. Sorta' like daydream sleep walking. I need to get going, the Burryman is about to leave."

"Oh, you're with the Burryman?"

"I am. I'm not doing a very good job though. I don't know how he does it."

"He has to have a great constitution, that's for sure," the man said. "Ok if I buy you a drink?"

"Thank you, really, but I'm married."

"Oh, is your husband here with you?"

"No, he couldn't make the trip."

The man nodded his head as if he somehow understood. "Ok, let me buy you a Heverlee just so you know that we are friendly to our guests."

Scara took a look over at the Burryman and he didn't seem quite ready to leave the bar; this would set them behind a few minutes, and replied, "Ok, what's a Heverlee?"

"It's a Belgian beer, a little on the sweet side," the man replied.

"That sounds good," Scara replied. She welcomed the reprieve from the horrors of the day. Were they only horrors of her mind or something more?

The sound of pool balls being racked at the billiard tables moved Scara's mind to Jeff. He used to be an avid pool player and he showed her a thing or two while they were dating. The smell of whisky was everywhere. She watched as the Burryman teetered a bit. It looked as if he may be ready to move on soon. Taking shots of whisky in a bar with a few hours left on his march might not be the best of ideas. The man came back with a frosty mug in his hand. He handed it over to Scara and she moved it to her lips. The man was right; the first thing she tasted was sweetness. It wasn't too sweet; it was just the right amount. The next taste of Heverlee was a healthy gulp; Scara didn't realize how thirsty she had become.

"Thank you," said Scara.

"My pleasure," replied the man.

Scara took another big gulp and motioned toward the Burryman.

"I think he's ready to move on, thank you for the beer, I'm sorry, I didn't get your name."

"Name is Sean, and yours?"

"Scara. I gotta' go."

She stood and followed the Burryman and company out the door. Sean smiled as he watched the woman leave. He let his mind wonder what her story was.

Next stop was The High Street.

August 9, 2020: 4:20 PM – The High Street

The bell-ringers rang the bells and Scara had become more of a traveling spectator than an active participant. This was the longest day of her life. Scara was happy to see a somewhat familiar place. It was time to stop at the High Street hotel, the very hotel where she was staying. Maybe she would get a chance to run up to her room. She needed to splash water on her face and recharge her batteries a little. The rooms were like apartments really; equipped with a spacious living area complete with a gas fireplace.

The Burryman was wobbly in the hotel lobby. Andrew was finally thinking that maybe he had bitten off more than he could chew. It was an honor but it was an honor that was going to take some getting used to if he were going to don the suit for the next few years. He was doing well to just stay focused on the routes and keep from falling over but he noticed something wasn't right with his new American friend. He was restricted from speaking but it didn't stop him from spinning around to see if he could put his slitted eyes on the shapely black haired woman that dined with him the night before. He was about to give up and get ready to move on to Honeypot Ceramics with the crew when he felt the tug on his left arm. Scara was smiling at him. She patted his arm and grabbed the bell from her reliever. She signed on for this so she was doing her best to finish it. The quick room break seemed to help Scara to focus. She was able to wash her face, brush her teeth and get an ice cold bottled water from the fridge. When she reappeared, the men in the lobby were certainly paying her attention that was for sure. She was getting this attention at every stop but her mind had been so preoccupied that this was the first time she really noticed it. It made her uncomfortable and smile at the same time. Jeff popped into her mind and quelled the smile. It came right back when she grabbed The Burryman by the arm.

"Ok, let's go," Scara said and helped guide him. George saw her and said, "I thought we lost you, young lady. I'm glad you didn't abandon the journey."

"I've got too much invested in it now," Scara smiled as she replied.

"I should say you do," George said.

CHAPTER 21

South Queensferry

Scara took a deep breath and opened the window; she saw the children playing. The air was fresh. She waved at them and felt the breeze catch her hair. Scara grabbed her cup of coffee and took a seat at the kitchen table. She was taking short sips when Jeff walked into the room.

"Mornin', babe," Jeff said after letting out a yawn.

"I was trying to be quiet, thought you might want to sleep late."

"Sleep late? No way, babe. We're in fuckin' Scotland, I don't want to sleep late. I'm raring to go."

"So, what's the plan of the day?" Scara asked and winked at her husband.

"The plan is something special."

"Special, really?"

"Kira, what time is it?"

"Almost eight, why?"

"Because we have to be somewhere at nine."

"Really? Where would that be?"

"Mum's the word, it's a surprise."

"You're lucky that I like surprises," Scara replied to her loving man.

"Bullshit, you hate surprises but I hope you like this one."

"Are we going to herd goats or something?"

"How'd you guess?"

"We're not herding goats..."

"Of course not. We got an hour to get ready. You want to meet me in the boudoir?"

"Of course I do," Scara replied. "Get on in there."

"Just let me grab a glass of water real quick," Jeff replied. Scara smiled at her muscular husband and went to the bedroom.

After their quick love making workout, they took a shower together and started to dress for the day.

"Kira, you don't need to get all made up. We're going to be doing a lot of walking today."

"Really? Now, the more you talk, the more curious I become."

"Wear your joggers, you'll thank me later." Jeff smiled at his wife.

The two walked out of the hotel hand in hand thirty minutes later.

"There it is," Jeff pointed.

"The Stag Head?"

"That's the place."

Scara got nervous all of a sudden and stopped in her tracks.

"I, I don't want to go in there," she said.

"Oh, honey, you're going to ruin the surprise. He's waiting on us," Jeff said.

The playing children all stopped, turned toward them and pointed. They began shouting.

"HIP, HIP HOORAY! IT'S THE BURRYMAN'S DAY! HIP, HIP HOORAY! IT'S THE BURRYMAN'S DAY!"

Jeff pulled Scara by the hand and she resisted.

"Jeff, I don't want to go in there," Scara moved back and Jeff's grip became tighter. Then he urged her along.

"You can't ruin the surprise, Kira."

Scara looked over her shoulder and the crowd was amassing behind her. It seemed as if all of South Queensferry was gathering and they joined the children in the chant.

"HIP, HIP HOORAY! IT'S THE BURRYMAN'S DAY! HIP, HIP HOORAY! IT'S THE BURRYMAN'S DAY!"

Scara was now being drug along. She wanted to plant her feet but felt the crowd closing in behind her. She could feel the hands of children touching her hair. The cobblestone street felt like she was balancing on boulders because every step came with a begrudging sense of despair that grew with every inch she moved toward the entrance of the Stag Head.

"HIP, HIP HOORAY! IT'S THE BURRYMAN'S DAY!"

They were in front of the door and Jeff let go of her hand. Scara's instinct was to turn and run but she knew the horde was waiting. There she was, standing in front of the stark white building. The building itself didn't seem very big on the outside and the front door was amber lit. Scara felt as if she may be standing in an entryway to Hell. She felt the breath of the people behind her. They were crowding her; threatening to consume her if she didn't move. Scara opened the door and stepped inside.

The room was dimly lit and she saw him in the center of it. There was a man to his left and right, holding the staves as the Burryman's arms was stuck straight out by his sides.

"Why am I here?" Scara found herself asking.

The Burryman looked at her. He didn't speak. He looked at her and Scara felt the tickle in her mind.

"You're here to give it to me. You're here to relieve yourself of the burden. You're here to give yourself to the silence. I will take it away but you have a price to pay the Burryman. Embrace the silence and I will take the guilt, I will take the pain."

Scara moved closer to the Burryman. The eye slits glowed a bright yellow as if the sun was going to burst from inside of the mask. She reached and grabbed him by the shoulders. Now, she was going to look directly into his eyes. She would look and he would release her. Scara looked and she woke up, dazed in the crowd.

"Scara," George was standing in front of her. Scara had her hands on his shoulders.

"What?"

"Are you ok? You were in some sort of trance for a spell."

"Oh my, I'm sorry. I don't know what came over me."

"You're not used to this sort of day of traipsing around and taking whisky. You want an escort back to High Street? You should lie down," he said.

"No, I'll be fine. Just need a glass of water and I'll be good to go."

"Well, if you zone out on us again, I'm going to have to send you back. I don't want anything to happen to our guest. That would be a terrible thing."

Maisie's Boutique – South Queensferry

George kept an eye on Scara for a bit after her extended daydreaming spell but his attention was quickly drawn back to supporting The Burryman.

The end of the march was near. Scara had left the snaggle-tooths behind a few stops ago; her mind was fucking with her – and so was the silence.

Maisie's Boutique was a welcome sight. The storefront was painted teal on white brick with the name of the shop **MAISIE'S BOUTIQUE**, lettered in white against the teal backdrop. It gave Scara a feeling of familiarity and comfort as soon as she walked inside. The bell-ringers bellowed outside while the Burryman sipped his whisky. Scara took this opportunity to duck inside of the gift shop for a quick perusal. She was met at the door by a pretty dark haired young woman.

"Hello, there, my name is Caley, I'm one of the Maisie gals," she said as she extended her hand with a wide smile on her face.

"Hi, I'm Scara."

"You with the Burryman's crew?"

"I am."

"Your accent? You're from the US, correct?"

"I am, I'm from Georgia, the peach state."

"Well, that's wonderful. I'm glad you got to participate in the Burryman's march. Been a long day for you, I'd imagine."

"You could say that," Scara replied. "I really like your store. Everything looks wonderful."

"Thank you; we opened our doors in 2007. We've been hanging in there but in between horrendous weather, even for Scotland, road works, gas works, cruise ships and the impending doom that is Brexit our little shop has been kind of quiet so we really need the favor of the Burryman," Caley said without skipping a beat.

"I understand the road work, gas work and cruise ship stuff but what is Brexit? I'm afraid I'm not up on foreig...well; I guess to you they would be domestic affairs. I apologize," Scara said sheepishly, a little embarrassed that she didn't know what Brexit was or why it was important.

"Well, in a nutshell it is the UK's exit from the European Union. What's at stake for us is national sovereignty, really. So, is Britain going to be ruled from Westminster, which has a parliament democratically elected by the people, or from Brussels, which is comprised of self designated bureaucrats of the European Union. The EU is controlled by Germany and France," Caley finished because she could see the strain in Scara's face, trying to understand the concept that is Brexit. "Anyway, you're from the States, so I'm sure you all have your own set of problems."

"Yeah, you could say that," Scara agreed. Her mind was still trying to figure out Brexit and that felt good. She wasn't preoccupied, she was in the moment having a thoughtful conversation with one of the Maisie Gals.

"So, you need to take anything back home? A knickknack or two?" Caley asked as she widened her arms out to the shop floor. "We have a little bit of everything."

Scara's face lit up and she gravitated to a table filled with candles. The lid labels all read in big, bold letters, **JUICY CANDLE!** And they each had different scents; like Cranberry Supreme, Pomegranate Cider, the list went on and on.

"I'll leave you to look around. You want me to let you know when the Burryman moves on?" Caley asked.

"No, that's ok; I'll catch up to them. I am fascinated by your store," Scara picked up two of the **JUICY CANDLES**, a Cranberry Supreme and a Salted Caramel & Pistachio, she was certain that her mother and sister would love them if she could get them back home.

The store wasn't huge in square footage but the Maisie Gals utilized every inch of available space. There were the cutest rubber galoshes in a variety of colors, surely attributed to the weather that Caley had mentioned. There were floral purses, Scara normally wasn't a floral purse kind of girl but one of them caught her fancy. These purses were labeled as painted and pressed so the detail in them was exquisite. The one in particular that caught her eye had a yellow, purple, pink and green floral arrangement painted on the black material of the purse. There were gift cards, costume jewelry, bags, games and trinkets, shot glasses, something called punky pins, bath salts, meditation soaps, stuffed animals, mugs, and balloons. Scara was truly shocked at the variety of merchandise in this small gift shop and she admired the Maisie Gals for organizing it in such a way so that you could navigate the store comfortably. Scara looked out of the front window – the Burryman and bell-ringers were still there and so was the line of people, some with hands full of burrs so Scara continued to look around. There was a large standing wooden shelf painted a pastel, Eastery, looking yellow. There were brightly colored bottles, tubes and jars on each shelf. Scara moved closer to make out what they were.

"Wow," Scara whispered. There was a mountain of Bettyhula moisturizing products laid out before her. The Bettyhula girl was on every one of them. The words, *Honest Natural Beauty*, were printed above Bettyhula. Scara reached for one of the tubes of hand moisturizer at the back of the third shelf, it was the only one she saw in the hot pink tube. She was transfixed for a moment by Bettyhula. She was a simply drawn, long haired beauty wearing a hula skirt (of course) and rubbing her hands, probably with the Rum & Blackcurrant anti-bacterial hand moisturizer, is what Scara imagined.

"That's our most popular," Caley said from across the room. "I thought we were out of those."

"It's the last one, it was stuck in the back," Scara replied.

"Take a drop, it's fine," Caley said and turned toward an approaching customer with a question already forming on their lips.

Scara unscrewed the cap and applied a small dollop to her palm. She didn't even have to raise her hand as the scent raced its way up Scara's face.

"Oh wow, that stuff smells so good," Scara said.

Caley approached.

"Yeah, I have a mini stock of it at my house. We sell the soap and the larger jars too but we can't keep this particular scent in stock."

"I can see why. I'll take the one tube. Wish you had more of this," Scara said.

"Why don't you smell the others? They all smell very good but you did pick the best one so you may have set the bar too high for your nose," Caley said.

"I've never seen this brand before," Scara said as she sampled a couple of other scents and Caley was spot on, they smelled good but not as good.

"I feel like I should be eating these. I've never seen this brand in the United States. I hope they have a website."

"We have a website, so you can order from us if you'd like, I'll save you some of the Rum & Blackcurrant when we replenish our stock. Just jot down your address and I'll send it to you as soon as we get it. Should have another shipment in about six or seven days," Caley said.

"Would you, really? That would be so great. My mother will fall in love with this stuff and I'll have to beat my sister away if she gets even one sniff of it." Scara was finally feeling somewhat relieved. It almost felt like she was on vacation.

"Well, we would have had more if we didn't have another visitor earlier today. She bought up all of the Rum & Blackcurrant, guess she missed that one," Caley said. Scara half listened as she jotted her address on a piece of the Maisie's stationary that Caley passed her.

"Well, that's just my luck; I'll get the purse and these." Scara grabbed a variety of other scents from the shelf and walked in Caley's direction. Scara stopped and everything she had in her arms fell to the floor.

"You ok? What's wrong?" Caley quickly moved toward Scara. Scara was pointing at the window.

"How could, where...where?" was all that would escape her lips. She was shocked back into her nightmare. The moment of reprieve she felt in this shop was snatched away and Scara was frightened. Caley grabbed her by the hand.

"It's ok, come sit, I'll get you a glass of water."

"How?" Scara was in a state of shock. There was no way she could have seen who she thought she had seen. No fucking way. She took a long swallow of the bottled water that Caley handed over and looked back at the window. The Burryman was moving along with the bell-ringers. It was almost time to head back to Stag Head and end this dreadful day.

"You good?" Caley asked. She picked up everything that Scara had dropped and set it on the front counter.

"Yeah, I think the jet lag is finally catching up to me," Scara said. She was tired of having normalcy dangled in her face just long enough for her guard to relax only to get bitch slapped in the face with her continued delusional bullshit.

"I don't think the Burryman would mind too much if you missed the rest of the walk. It's practically over now, just one more stop and back to the Stag Head where I'm sure he is ready to shed that cumbersome costume. I don't see how they do it, really. It looks so heavy and uncomfortable," Caley said.

"I suppose you're right. I should go back to my room and lie down for a little while before I grab a bite. Let me pay for my stuff and I'll be on my way."

"Just sit another few minutes, love. Sit and make sure you are good to go before you leave. I don't want to turn on the telly and hear of a woman collapsing in the street after she left Maisie's Boutique; that would be bad for business," Caley said with a smile.

"I'll be fine, thank you so much; it was so cool meeting you, Caley. I got your card and your email so I'll be in touch when I get back home," Scara replied and grabbed the bag of goodies.

"You take care of yourself, Scara and I hope you enjoy your time here in Queensferry." Caley waved and Scara exited the shop.

Scara kept looking over her shoulder as she skipped past the Burryman's crew at the Orocco Pier. She walked straight to the Stag Head. She'd wait there to see how Andrew was holding up.

August 9, 2020: 6:00 PM – Stag Head

George tugged on the costume from the back and the bell-ringers helped remove the mask. Andrew's puffy, red face emerged and his eyes were a little glazed over.

"Get him some water," George grunted to anyone that would listen. Cameron gave the salute, grabbed the closest stein he could get his hands on and filled it to the brim with ice followed by straight tap water. He held it out to Andrew whose arms were just freed. Andrew greedily lifted the stein to his lips and took slow, deliberate swallows. He knew better than to take long, fast gulps, which would have been very painful after all of the walking and drinking he had done that day.

"Scara, what happened to her?" was his first question after he finished the stein.

"She was feeling poorly for a good bit of the walk, I think she may have gone on ahead to lie down. I don't think the poor girl knew what she was in for when we started off this morning," George said.

"Cameron, can you go over to High Street and check on her for me in a bit?" Andrew asked.

"Yeah, anything Andrew. You did a great job for your first time. You held your whisky better than I though you might," Cameron said as he made his way to the front door. He reached to open it when it was pushed open from the other side. It was Scara.

"I found her!" Cameron turned and announced full of jest.

"Scara, hey," Andrew said. Scara could see that he was physically exhausted from the half wave of his arm when he spoke.

"Hey, Andrew. You did so good," Scara started. "I guess I wasn't quite in the shape I thought I was. I'm sorry about that."

"I couldn't see you very well in the suit. I could hear you from time to time and after a while I just stopped hearing you at all. George said you had a little difficulty during the march but it's, as they say, all good," Andrew said.

"Yeah, he's not wrong. I wasn't feeling too good at a couple of the stops. Truth be told, I found myself fascinated with Maisie's Boutique and I just lingered there a little longer than I expected. I made a few purchases, talked to a Maisie Gal and when I came outside, you all had moved on."

"Maisie's Boutique is a beautiful shop, it's amazing how much they can fit in that space," Andrew said.

"I know, right?" Scara replied.

"Well, I'm glad you're ok. I will be going back to my flat and soaking in a hot bath. The Ferry Fair kicks off tomorrow."

"It has been a very long day, I'm going back to the hotel and soak my dogs, order some room service and make sure I'm bright eyed and bushy tailed for the Ferry Fair tomorrow. George?"

"Yes, my dear?" he asked.

"You want to come by my hotel in a little while and give me a Ferry Fair lesson?" Scara asked.

"It would be my pleasure to meet a beautiful lady like yourself at her hotel," George said with a wink.

I KNOW I WILL DIE IN THE SILENCE – THE BURRYMAN

"I'll meet you at the bar at seven thirty. Will that work?" Scara asked.

"It will," he smiled.

"And Andrew?"

"Yes, my dear?" he replied mimicking George's voice.

"Will you meet me at my hotel in the morning? I'd like you to spend the first day of the Ferry Fair with me if I'm not being too bold."

"Your wish is my command," Andrew replied. "Now, you may want to leave. I'm going to take the lower part of the costume off and I have nothing on underneath."

"Hmmm, maybe I'll stay for a few minutes." Scara laughed as she paused at the door. She stopped for a second as she caught the glimpse of another. It was quick and her mind was working to convince her otherwise. *No way, can't be,* is what she thought when she made herself leave so her new friends wouldn't think she was losing her mind. Scara thought maybe that was exactly what was happening; maybe the silence was coming to collect its debt.

———

Melissa spun around and moved to the back of the room when she saw Scara standing in the doorway. Had she been spotted? She wasn't sure if she got out of sight quickly enough and waited to see if Scara would cut through the room and face up to her. She braced herself, hoping she wouldn't have the confrontation right there and then but she wouldn't run from it if Scara approached. Melissa steeled herself for a tap on the shoulder. It didn't come. She turned around, peeked around the corner and Scara was gone.

CHAPTER 22

August 9, 2020: 8:45 PM – High Street

Scara was fascinated by George and she hated that she cut his Ferry Fair lesson short when he met her promptly at 7:30 but Scara was plum tired. She thought hard about cutting her trip short. Just change the flight and get her ass back to Atlanta, back to her Mama and Lisa. Call Jeff, hear his voice. Pet her cat. The visions of the day, the snaggle toothed monstrosities conjured by her guilty mind. Sleep came quickly and that's when the silence came at her again.

"HIP, HIP HOORAY! IT'S THE BURRYMAN'S DAY!"

And there he was. He was lumbering toward her in a field of green. The sun was setting and Scara could feel the breeze in her hair. She was taking long, measured breaths as if they may be the last few that she drew. The grass was tall and waving in the wind. The Burryman was moving slowly toward her and the sky carried the chant. There were no bell-ringers to be seen. There were no crowds lined up with burrs and whisky. The Burryman was steady in his approach. His arms were outstretched with staves in each hand. There were no assistants. It was just him.

Scara heard him for the first time. It wasn't Andrew's voice. The Burryman spoke slowly.

"I'm here for you. I'm here to take it all away. Just place your burrs and give me whisky…I'll take it away from you. I'll bear it and you can finally have silence."

"I, I don't want silence. I want to live. I'm a horrible person; I shouldn't have let Jeff take the fall for me. I shouldn't have left Melissa the way that I did. I should have just called the police when Johnny started messing with me again. I should have done a lot of things differently." Scara's voice cracked. The Burryman was standing in front of her now. He seemed to be ten feet tall. His face was dark and the burrs stuck out everywhere. Scara could hardly make out the narrow eye slits. She fell to her knees in front of him as if she were praying to an idol for salvation. She thrust her hands into the grass almost expecting the blades to cut her and she felt for them. They were everywhere at the base of the blades. Scara scooped up two handfuls of burrs and looked up at the Burryman. Her eyes were pleading.

"Place them and you will have your life. Place them, Scara. That's all you have to do."

Scara stood up on shaky legs and began to stretch out her arms. She extended the burrs closer to the lumbering giant. He was looking down upon her. The chants of, "HIP, HIP HOORAY! IT'S THE BURRYMAN'S DAY!" were almost deafening. Scara's hands trembled as the burrs were within an inch of touching the Burryman. She looked up at him and opened her hands. The burrs fell back into the grass. Scara woke up shaking.

"Shit...fuck," Scara mumbled, got up and turned on the shower. The shower was more for comfort than cleanliness. She would take the hot shower, and then hopefully be able to get a couple of hours of sleep and be ready for Andrew. Scara remembered her dream; it wasn't something vague or a fog in her mind, she remembered it vividly and wondered exactly what would have happened had she placed the burrs. Scara seriously pondered if she would have woken up or if the silence would have swallowed her whole. Scara would take her shower and go back to bed. Sleep came back to her and kept her until she woke up and things were turned upside down.

Scara felt groggy. Something wasn't right. She tried to sit up and she felt the strain of resistance on her wrists and ankles. A queer thought came to her even as she came to the realization that she couldn't sit up in the bed. Today was the first day of the Ferry Fair and she would hate to miss it.

"Hello, Kira," she heard the voice say. The room was still dark but daylight had already broken. She saw the figure standing pat on the far side of the room.

"Jeff?" Scara asked. She knew it wasn't Jeff but it was Jeff's word for her, Kira, that made the question leap from her mouth.

"It's the Burryman, Kira. It's the Burryman and I've come to deliver the silence."

"What?" Scara pulled again and felt the restraints. Scara screamed, "LET ME GO!!! HELP!!!"

"Don't you feel it?"

"Feel what? What am I supposed to feel?"

"Be quiet, Kira, just feel it."

The room seemed to be rocking softly. Scara focused her eyes onto the figure as he moved. She could see the light coming through. It was natural sunlight.

"Do you realize where you are?"

"Look, I don't know who you are..."

"You don't know who I am, Kira?"

"The Burryman," Scara whispered. She was shaking.

Morning of the Ferry Fair – South Queensferry

Claire grabbed Melissa gently by the crook of her arm as if she were being walked into the prom.

"Hey, girl I lost you for a bit."

"Oh, hey, I tend to get distracted very easily, you know like a dog eyeballing a squirrel?"

"A dog eyeballing a squirrel, you say? I'll have to remember that one," Claire replied.

"It's just an expression where I'm from," Melissa said.

"Well, undistract yourself; we have a busy day today. It's the first day of the Ferry Fair," Claire said.

"Are those storm clouds?" Melissa tugged at her shirt as she asked. She squirmed a little while making the adjustment. The shirt was just a tad too tight.

"If one pops up, we will dip in one of the shops until it passes," Claire reassured.

"Sounds like a plan, but I need to stop over at the High Street Hotel real quick before we start our day. Let me walk over there and I'll meet you back here in an hour," Melissa said as casually as she would if she had lived there all of her life.

"I'll walk with you, Melissa. What on earth could you need at the High Street?"

"I told somebody back home that I would check something out for them and it's somewhat of a personal request so I would rather go alone if it's all the same to you," Melissa said with the same casual tone.

"Ok," Claire replied. She wouldn't push it with her new friend. Everyone had their quirks, she supposed.

Melissa took a deep breath as she approached the High Street's entrance. She stepped inside and immediately saw an older woman smiling at her from behind a nondescript counter.

"Yes, young lady. How may I help you?" the woman asked. Her hair was dyed black and was probably the color of the youth that she was desperately trying to pull back.

"Hi, I was wondering if a note was left for *M.B.* It should just have those initials," Melissa said.

The woman looked back at her as if requests for initialized notes happened everyday and replied, "Yes, there is a note here for *M.B.* But on the back of the note, it says please do not give it to the person asking unless he or she knows the keyword," the woman said. She seemed to be getting some enjoyment out of this. The woman was thinking what a clever game this young lady's lover or husband was playing with her. Secret notes at High Street, probably revealing the room number for their tryst. A wonderful fantasy which she was now a part. She was the keeper of the note and if the young lady didn't know the answer, maybe the older lady would go up and surprise the young beau.

"Augusta, the keyword is Augusta."

The woman nodded her head and feigned disappointment as she handed the note over. She expected the young woman to open it right there and bolt off to a room. The young woman did neither. She turned her back and walked out of the High Street leaving the older woman's fantasy shattered.

Two hours passed and Claire hadn't heard a word from Melissa. She was afraid that her new friend had stood her up. Claire wanted to worry about Melissa but something was off. She didn't feel worried for her at all. There was an air of confidence Melissa conveyed that made Claire think Melissa knew exactly what she was doing; that Melissa had really come here for a purpose and that purpose wasn't to finish a thesis on the Ferry Fair. Claire began to think that maybe she should just stay out of Melissa's business. Claire walked away to start her day at the Ferry Fair. She would never see Melissa again.

Orocco Pier

Melissa pulled the note from her pocket and took a moment to inhale a full, deep breath of fresh ocean air. The Shore Walk is what Melissa wanted to take (she just didn't have the time), a nice leisurely four and a half mile stroll from South Queensferry to neighboring Cramond for what many call the most beautiful coastal line that you will see on the planet. She opened the note.

Package received. You were correct, she didn't change the reservations, no issues. Will arrive at 9:00 AM for pickup.

Melissa glanced at her phone and it was 8:52. She looked toward the end of the pier and saw the boat approaching. She moved quickly and as soon as she reached the end of pier, the boat was positioned as to where she could step right on board. It paused only to pick her up.

"Glad you could make it," said a deep voice.

"I couldn't miss it," Melissa replied as the boat pulled away from the pier as quickly as it had approached. It was off to open water; off to silence.

———————

The sudden jolt brought Scara around. She was having dreams of snaggle-toothed children pointing at her; shouting the arrival of the Burryman. Scara could feel the movement; the sound of water. They were slicing through the still ocean; she could feel the rhythm of the boat's stern slapping water as it cruised. It was coming back to her. She tried to sit up and screamed.

"LET ME GO!!!!" Scara shouted. Her throat was hoarse and she suddenly found herself very thirsty. She burst into tears when she heard the woman reply.

"Hey, Scara."

"Melissa?"

"Yeah, it's me."

"It was you, it was you I saw, that was real…what, what are you doing here?" Scara was as confused as she had ever been.

"I booked the trip after some deep contemplation. I couldn't get past you leaving me to die in the dark water of Clarks Hill Lake," Melissa said with the southern twang that Scara once thought was endearing but now it was just menacing.

"I thought we put this behind us, Melissa. I really did. I apologized to you. I didn't know what to do. I know, I know I didn't do the right thing. If I could go back and change it, I would."

"Well, maybe I can test that theory," Melissa replied. A puzzled look covered Scara's face. "Where is he?" Scara asked.

"Where is who?" Melissa replied.

"Don't fuck with me Melissa. How did Johnny escape too? How did he get out of the country? How did he get you to help him? What did he say to you?" Scara could now see Melissa completely. She noticed that her hair was longer and her face was thinner.

Melissa had lost a few pounds since the last time they'd seen each other and Scara figured it wasn't the good kind of losing weight. It was the almost getting drowned to death and freaking the fuck out over the one that almost killed you losing weight.

"Johnny, dipshit, Pickens? That the Johnny you referring to, Scara? I'm afraid that whatever might be left of old Johnny is still floating around in teeny tiny pieces back at Clarks Hill. He's dead as far as I know."

"Who's helping you?" Scara's lips began to quiver. She could feel the silence marching toward her. She could feel the Burryman coming to take her away; remove the burden of sin that was her albatross.

"I got a pen pal after that night, Scara. I had some things to get off of my chest. You know, a confession to make," Melissa moved closer to Scara.

Scara could tell the boat was no longer accelerating. It was just floating along.

Then, there he was, covered in burrs and breathing heavily through the mask.

"It started with one letter. I had to let him know what kind of person he wanted to spend his life with," Melissa knelt down close to Scara's ear and whispered, "I made it my mission to get him out. I got him out. He has a new name. He has a new life. And this little country hick girl did it. I wish you didn't leave me to die, Scara. We should have been forever friends," Melissa finished, planted a gentle kiss on Scara's cheek and backed away.

Scara knew what Melissa was saying but it couldn't be true. She would have heard about it. Maybe she should have taken that last phone call.

"Is it really you?" Scara asked the figure.

"I'm the Burryman, Kira. I'm here to take you for the greater good. You let people lie to protect you. You throw people away to protect yourself. The silence of the deep is here for you now."

Melissa unstrapped the restraints as the Burryman continued.

"You didn't cancel this trip and you told yourself it was because you wanted to recharge. You told yourself that you were a good person. You believed it. But, you know the truth and over time, I learned the truth. When you didn't answer the calls with the frequency you used to. When you knew that I loved you with everything that I had and more."

"No, it can't be you. I'm so sorry, I'm so sorry, babe. I love you more than anything. I'd do anything for you."

"Well," the Burryman began as he pulled the mask from his face, "like Melissa said; now you can prove it."

"Oh My GOD!" Scara screamed. It was Jeff but it wasn't. His face had changed. He looked older and she could see the fresh ink of tattoos that went up the sides of his neck.

"She told me everything, Kira. I didn't want to believe it. I tore up the first letter after I read it. I didn't want to believe what I was reading. I tore it up and I called you. I called you and you didn't answer. I called you again and you didn't answer but you know what I did get? I got letters from Melissa letting me know exactly what you'd done. I was happy to hear that you sent Johnny to his grave but Melissa was caught up in your shit just like I was. I was obligated to fall for you, at least that's what I thought, but she wasn't. Kira, it's time for you to prove you can take the silence. It's time for you to sink or swim."

"No, Jeff, please don't do this, you don't want to do this!" Scara screamed. Melissa stood quietly as Jeff lifted her from the bed. Her body was weak but she slapped at his face and punched at his chest as best she could. Jeff carried her up the steps just like he carried her over the threshold when they moved into their home.

Melissa stayed put. She heard the splash and she could hear Scara screaming and struggling until she couldn't.

Jeff came back down the stairs.

"Help me get this fucking thing off," he said.

"Do you think she'll make it?" Melissa asked.

"Maybe. You did. If she makes it, we'll all go back together. If she doesn't then it wasn't meant to be. You know the Burryman festival was going to be my surprise for her. This shit is so fucked up," Jeff said and Melissa gave him a long kiss.

"I hope she makes it then we can all start fresh," Melissa said and grabbed Jeff by the hand.

"Me too," Jeff replied.

———

Scara felt the coldness blanket her like a newborn. There was nothing but silence. It was finally time. It wasn't exactly how she had imagined but the silence did come for Scara. The silence stroked her black hair with waves of dark water; caressing her like her mother used to when she was a child. She kicked for the light. She heard Joey laughing somewhere. The silence was comforting her as she felt her lungs give up the fight. It was beckoning her. She blinked her eyes and saw the light dwindling above her but everything was ok. She could see Joey; he was waving her in. Scara was where she always knew she would be. She knew that she would die in the silence and the Burryman washed away the guilt. Scara smiled as water filled her lungs. She was chanting in her mind, HIP, HIP HOORAY! IT'S THE BURRYMAN'S DAY! Then, there was light.

EPILOGUE

One year later.

Jeff Slayfield was now Chad Simmons. He was living in Charlotte, NC with his wife, Melissa. She had just found out the week before that she was pregnant. Chad worked as an auto mechanic at **Spike's Tire & Lube**. He could turn a wrench and had a knack for identifying engine trouble through his ears rather than diagnostic machines – machines that showed diagnosed problem(s) were almost always caused by another issue. In most cases, Chad could quickly identify the other issue.

Melissa secured a job at a local daycare and thought it would be perfect for her with the baby coming and all. Great practice with other people's kids is what she thought. The pair rented a home just outside of downtown Charlotte. They lived in a quiet neighborhood with a fenced in backyard. They both looked forward to their new life together. They even had a brown and white cat that Chad affectionately named Kira. The two of them had arrived home at just about the same time on this rainy Thursday evening. The sky was dark and thunder grumbled in the sky.

"It's going to be a shit-storm tonight, babe," Chad said as he brushed his feet on the welcome mat before stepping into the house.

"Make sure you don't let Kira outside, she might get skittish and go tree climbing before it really gets bad," Melissa said as she removed her jacket.

"What's for dinner, babe?"

"Frozen pizza, I didn't put anything out to thaw and was running too late to throw something in the crock pot unless you want to order delivery," Melissa said and shrugged her shoulders.

"That would be kind of a dick move with the storm-front moving in, frozen pizza is fine," Chad said.

"I'll make it up to you later," Melissa said.

"Is that right?" Chad replied and moved toward the kitchen closet – that's where they kept Kira's kibble. The cat was in the kitchen lickety-split as soon as she heard the closet door open. "Damn girl, you starving?" Chad smiled at Kira and reached down to pet her. Kira arched her back and hissed. "Ok, don't be bitchy about it, here's your food." Chad filled her bowl and only then did Kira let him pet her.

"Smart girl, no play until you pay," Melissa said and went to the freezer.

"How's the morning sickness? Better? Worse? You up for a little rainy night lovin'?"

"Not bad today and of course, I am."

Melissa set the oven to four hundred degrees, popped the pizza in and they waited twenty minutes before she pulled it out and they dined on a circle of something that tasted like cardboard with what passed as mozzarella on top.

The storm picked up shortly after dinner and the power was knocked out. The wind was howling and Kira was hiding under the recliner in the living room. It was on their list to buy a generator for situations exactly like this but they hadn't gotten around to it because they hadn't saved the necessary funds. Their Queensferry trip was expensive.

They conserved hot water by showering together and then they began making love just as the storm outside intensified.

———————

Four hours later.

The storm was in for the long haul and the house was cloaked in darkness. The rain pounded the roof and the wind threatened to peel up shingles.

Chad and Melissa were fast asleep. Melissa was dreaming of the silence – the cold water as her lungs were on the verge of exploding. She could see Scara smiling at her. The silence was coming for her. Claire told her about the Burryman. Did Scara have to die for what she did?

Guilt is a curious creature; it burrows under your skin and sleeps. It sleeps and begins to grow as it slowly awakens.

The Burryman was the scapegoat. He could take the guilt.

Melissa could hear Scara scream as her loving husband tossed her over the side. Scara was screaming. She was too weak to swim away; she was taken by the silence.

Thunder boomed and lightning cracked the sky. Melissa sat up in the bed, her heart was pounding. She reached over to shake Chad awake. He wasn't there. There was a wet spot on his side of the bed. Melissa reached for the bedside table and clicked the lamp. The room remained dark.

"Shit, shit, shit," Melissa threw the covers back and grabbed her phone and shined it on Chad's side, expecting to see blood soaked sheets but they were just wet; it was only water. Melissa, just realizing that she was naked, threw on the robe that was hanging on the bedpost.

"Please, please, please," Melissa repeated as she moved precariously down the hallway. She took measured steps as if she were on a high wire connected to opposing New York City skyscrapers. She paused before turning the corner into the living room. She could hear shutters slamming and could feel the force of the wind shooting around the corner. The front door was wide open. "Please, please, please," Melissa continued her whisper. She was dialing 911 and the thunder boomed again, the lightning soon followed and lit up the sky, painting a ghastly portrait. It was like a Polaroid frozen in time. In the flash, Melissa saw Chad lying face down on the floor. Kira the cat was beside him and they were both motionless.

"Shit, shit, shit," Melissa dialed 911. The operator answered almost immediately. "911, what's your emergency?"

The lightning flashed again and Melissa dropped the phone. The figure of a shapely woman and a menacing monster stood in the doorway. Melissa was frozen in place. The pair moved toward her.

"HIP, HIP HOORAY, IT'S THE BURRYMAN'S DAY!" the woman shouted.

"Scara...oh my God, Scara...what, how?" Melissa's eyes widened. The 911 operator was mumbling something from the floor but Melissa was locked in the silence. The lightning flashed again and the Burryman was in full view. He was a large man covered in a suit of burrs. The burrs looked as if they had turned black and his arms weren't stuck at his sides. They reached out for Melissa.

"Just grab his hand and he'll take it all away," the woman said.

Melissa closed her eyes, wishing it were a dream but knowing it wasn't, and she took the hand of the Burryman. She felt his soothing grip and the release of her guilt just before the silence consumed her. Melissa would never hear her baby cry.

THE END